nothing can keep us together

a gossip girl novel

Gossip Girl novels by Cecily von Ziegesar:

nothing can keep us together
a gossip girl
novel

by

Cecily von Ziegesar

BLOOMSBURY

Published in Great Britain in 2005 by Bloomsbury Publishing Plc
36 Soho Square, London W1D 3QY

This edition published by arrangement with
Little, Brown & Company (Inc.), New York, NY, USA
All rights reserved

 Produced by 17th Street Productions,
an Alloy, Inc. company
151 West 26th Street, New York, NY 10001, USA

A CIP catalogue record of this book is available from the
British Library
ISBN 0 7475 7610 6
ISBN 9780747576105

All papers used by Bloomsbury Publishing are natural, recyclable
products made from wood grown in well-managed forests. The
manufacturing processes conform to the environmental
regulations of the country of origin.

Printed in Great Britain by Clays Ltd, St Ives plc

10 9 8 7 6 5 4 3

When caught between two evils, I generally like to take the one I never tried.

—Mae West

 gossipgirl.co.uk

Disclaimer: All the real names of places, people, and events have been altered or abbreviated to protect the innocent. Namely, me.

hey people!

June is right around the corner and New York City is like a burning Diptyque candle: hot and smelly, beautiful and bright. It's getting dark so late now, we can't tell the difference between night and day. Not that we care. At this time of year our turf—also known as the Upper East Side—is virtually parent-free. They're far too busy with polo matches and garden parties, tennis matches and golf games up at our country houses in Ridgefield, Connecticut; Bridgehampton, Long Island; Newport, Rhode Island; or Mt. Desert Isle, Maine, leaving us to rule the town. Not that we ever *stopped* ruling the town. Our names have been at the top of the guest list at every exclusive restaurant, club, and hotel in Manhattan since the day we were born. We move in clusters, dominating the scene uptown and downtown, east and west. The entire island is and always has been *ours*, but with June comes graduation, and for us seniors that means saying goodbye. But let's not get all sappy and dreary. Now's the time to really make our mark. If we get what we want for graduation, pretty soon we'll all have *cars*. It's our turn to be louder and more obnoxious and more beautiful than ever—honk, honk!! And with no one around to disapprove (as if we care), it's time to seriously misbehave.

Five reasons to party harder than we ever have in our lives:

1) Studying for finals is deathly boring.

2) It's almost summer!

3) We deserve it!!

4) The AC is cranked so high, we have to find *some* way to keep warm—nudge, nudge.

5) It's our last chance. Most of us will be going away for the summer, and after that, it's off to college. *This is it.*

Before you get too crazy and do something you might regret, you'll need to decide whether you and your boyfriend are devoted enough to have a long-distance relationship throughout the summer and on into college. Imagine yourself surrounded by tan hunks in Billabong surf shorts, with sandy bare feet, offering you rides in their vintage Cabriolets. Imagine hot campus prepsters in only their cute mint-green-and-white polka-dotted J.Crew boxers, on their way to the showers in your coed dorm. Will you honestly be able to resist? Why not save yourself the pain of a torturous, drawn-out breakup by breaking up now? Then treat yourself to a meaningless fling with that shy, adorable geek you went to ballroom dancing school with in fifth grade who's not such a geek anymore. You've got absolutely nothing to lose. And while you're at it, why not at least *pretend* to be nice to the stringy-haired, bucktoothed girl you forgot to invite to your birthday party in seventh grade and every birthday party you've had since. That way she can point to your picture in the yearbook and brag to all her new pals at Mt. Hollyhock or whatever dorky college she's going to next year, "See this cool chick here? She was one of my best friends!" But never mind trying to rekindle old romances and repair messed-up friendships.

I don't know about you, but I've got a major fashion crisis on my hands. Most of the private girls' schools take their graduation ceremonies extremely seriously. The girls must wear long white dresses, white gloves, and white shoes. It's like a wedding, except we're being set free instead of tied down—yippee! Still, the question looms: to Oscar or not to Oscar. Oscar de la Renta, that is. If you go for Oscar, you're likely to wind up wearing the same dress as six of your other classmates, although you know you're going to look far better in him than they do. And the nice thing about having to stick to white is that you can always dye it and wear it again. Yeah, right—like you're ever going to *want* to wear that dress again!

While I've got your attention, let's check in on a few of our favorite people. . . .

The odd couple

There has been some speculation that the relationship between those two totally opposite Williamsburg apartment sharers is not just a simple, convenient roommate situation but something more—how shall we put it?—*romantic.* **B** does seem to be wearing a lot of black lately, and her shoes are getting chunkier. And what was with that silver Tiffany *barrette* in **V**'s supershort hair the other day? Can't you just picture them, cuddling on the sofa, combing each other's hair, trading Manolos and Doc Martens? . . . Who needs boys?!

Speaking of boys

B may have given them up entirely—who wouldn't, after **N**'s latest stunt?—but **V** seems to be enjoying the company of the opposite sex more and more. She and **B**'s shaven-headed vegan step-brother, **A**, have been romping unfettered and partially clothed in coffee shops and on park benches all over Williamsburg. Nothing like a little PDA to light **V**'s fire!

As for **N**, you'd think he'd be on top of the world after scoring the city's most desirable blond bombshell—right in front of **B**, in the pool house bathtub during the girls' senior cut day party out in Southampton, no less. But no. Have you seen him lately? Red-rimmed eyes, dirty tissues streaming from his pockets, lackluster disposition. Our golden boy appears to be in a terrible funk. Or maybe he caught a sexually transmitted disease from one of those French tramps he's always rumored to be hooking up with. See? It doesn't pay to be too greedy. Not that that ever stopped us.

Your e-mail

Sightings

B and **V** buying potted basil plants at a **Williamsburg** farmer's market. Maybe the gay rumors about them are true!? **C** entering a **Greenwich Village** barbershop to have his head shaved and exiting with his hair longer than before and with platinum highlights. No way will he last even a month at military school. **N** standing on the roof of the Met, mournfully surveying **Central Park**. Looks like our favorite stoner playboy has been struck with a bad case of ennui. **D** checking out bashed-up Buicks at some seedy used car lot in **Harlem**. Not that he even knows how to operate a gearshift. **J** taking a solo SSAT—the boarding school admissions exam—on a Saturday in the headmistress's office at Constance Billard. She's determined to go, and her school is even more determined to get rid of her!

All you have to do is pass

My advice: Don't miss a Zac Posen sample sale or a Stella McCartney trunk show for one of those silly everything-we-ever-learned pre-final exam cram sessions the teachers "recommend" you attend after school. Do pour yourself a goblet of well-chilled pinot grigio and casually read through your notebooks. All you have to do is pass, and believe me, you're a lot smarter than you think. Good luck, my darlings. Can't wait to see you at graduation!

You know you love me.

gossip girl

where the girls all go

"Are you going to try that on?" a weirdly underdeveloped senior named Alison Baker asked Blair Waldorf timidly. Blair pushed the silver hanger down the rail toward Alison. A white, cardboard-stiff linen tunic by some random Scandinavian designer? *No, thanks.*

"Take it," she responded generously.

Alison had thin, waist-length brown hair, a gap between her front teeth, and was bone thin. She wore a white button-down oxford shirt every day and the type of navy blue lace-up shoes that Constance Billard required in kindergarten but which were phased out of the uniform in first grade. Once, in fourth grade, Alison had peed in her pants in the library because she wouldn't go to the bathroom before finishing *Anne of Green Gables*, and she'd had to spend the rest of the day wearing a pair of too-small mustard yellow cable-knit Hanna Andersson wool tights from the lost and found with no underwear.

Scratch, scratch.

In sixth grade, Alison had unsuccessfully invited Blair to her country house in Osterville on Cape Cod two weekends in a row before finally giving up. She'd then proceeded to spread a nasty rumor that Blair's father wouldn't let her go away on weekends because he and Blair were having an incestuous relationship and that was the only time they had together.

Blair's totally *gay* dad? Hello, stupidness?

"That dress would look fantastic on you. My shoulders are way too narrow for it," Blair lied.

Alison pulled the tunic dress on over her oxford shirt and let her Constance Billard uniform fall to the floor. The dress hung from her stick-figure body like a soggy potato sack. With her mousy brown hair in a limp middle part, she looked like the girl who gets possessed by a demon in that sick horror film *The Exorcist*. "Do you think it's too big?" she asked Blair.

Even Blair didn't have the heart to pretend that Alison actually looked good. "Maybe," she replied, too preoccupied with the pile of brightly colored, slinky silk jersey Diane von Furstenberg cami-dresses to care anymore.

"Hey, I was about to try that one on!" Isabel Coates whipped a frothy white Stella McCartney frock out of Rain Hoffstetter's hands and held it up to her ladder-tall, waistless frame. She was growing out her bangs and her sleek, dark hair was bobby-pinned down to her forehead in seven different places in a sort of intentional disarray that looked semi-cool and semiretarded.

"Hello? That's a size two. No *way* are you a size two," Rain countered, gripping the hem of the dress and threatening to rip it out of Isabel's hands. "I'm shorter than you," she insisted determinedly, even though, like Isabel, Rain was a lot closer to a size six than a size two.

"I don't know why you guys are being such bitches about that stupid dress," Blair yawned over at them as she moved on to a rack of beaded lilac-and-pink Sea Island cotton Nicole Farhi sweetheart sweaters. "It's *off*-white, and look." She pointed a pearly manicured finger at the white satin padded hanger the frock hung from. "The belt that goes with it is *pink*. Our graduation dresses have to be totally *white*."

Even though it was two sizes too small, Isabel still clung to the dress as if her life depended on it. "Well, maybe I don't want it for graduation. Maybe I have a party to go to or something."

As if she got invited to secret parties that Blair didn't know about.

Today was opening day for the Browns of London trunk show in the main ballroom at the St. Clair Hotel, and this particular group of Constance Billard senior girls had all cut homeroom to be there. What better way to find the dress that had been sampled in England but never sold in New York—the perfect, coveted, one-of-a-kind graduation dress. The only problem was that their graduation dresses had to be all white, and most designers shy away from all-white dresses so as not to invoke unsexy images of baby christenings and Little Bo Peep.

Not to mention wedding gowns.

"Too bad this one has a train," Kati Farkas mused, holding up a snowy, puffy-sleeved satin number by Alexander McQueen that looked like the dress Sleeping Beauty had worn to bed when she slept for a hundred years.

"*Ew*," Isabel sniffed. "The train is definitely not the only thing wrong with it."

The trunk show consisted of fifty-eight racks of dresses—including ball gowns, cocktail dresses, wedding and bridesmaid dresses, skirts, blouses, cardigans, and capri pants, two hat racks, and even a rack full of tiaras, veils, and scarves. The clothes were gorgeous and exquisitely made, but the girls were not being gentle with them. Clothes were strewn all over the claret-colored carpet, and the usually glamorous, gilt-accented ballroom looked like the walk-in closet of a fashion-crazed Upper East Side-dwelling Manhattan society hostess in a pre-getting-dressed-for-a-benefit alcoholic frenzy.

The throng of graduation-dress-hunting girls fell silent for a moment as a tall blond girl with enormous dark blue eyes pushed open the door to the ballroom and handed her white-and-green leather Louis Vuitton Calla Lily stuff sack over to security. Behind her stood a tanned boy with wavy golden brown hair and glittering green eyes.

"I bet they're late because they had to get a room first," Rain giggled, nudging Nicki Button in the ribs. Over the weekend, Rain and Nicki had gotten Japanese hair straightening treatments together, and their dark brown hair looked unnaturally straight and glossy, like it had been glued on by specialists from Madame Tussaud's wax museum in London.

"Look. Blair is totally pretending she didn't see them come in. Oh my God, and Serena is, like, walking right up to her!" Laura Salmon whispered shrilly.

Their arms full of dresses, the other girls followed Serena van der Woodsen with their eyes as she floated toward a rack of elegant-but-still-a-little-dorky straw sun hats two feet away from Blair and began to try them on.

"Nice," Nate Archibald commented unenthusiastically from where he slouched against the wall, looking more brooding and introspective than usual. This was the sort of trunk show where, instead of waiting in line forever for the two private changing rooms, most girls stripped down in between the racks to try things on. But Nate was the most desirable boy on the Upper East Side. Girls got naked at the snap of his stoned fingers, and it was still he who got ogled, not them. It was no surprise that he seemed unimpressed. It was also obvious from the way he kept his eyes trained on his limited edition Stan Smith tennis shoes that he was doing his best to pretend he hadn't noticed that Blair—the girl he was supposed to spend the rest of his life with but had fucked over only last week by fooling around with Serena on senior cut day—was standing only twenty feet away, glaring at him.

After walking in on Nate and Serena, Blair had sworn to herself that she would not freak out at the sight of them, grab the nearest sharp or heavy object, and hurl it at their heads, shouting, "Cheating, horny fuckheads!" But she couldn't help feeling more than a little pissed off by how good they looked together. The natural highlights in Nate's hair were exactly the same pale gold color as Serena's hair, and they both had the same healthy, sun-drenched glow, as if they'd spent hours together on a blanket in Sheep Meadow, kissing and getting tan. Serena was wearing one of Nate's weather-beaten navy blue short-sleeved polo shirts, its collar faded and the hem frayed, and Nate's cheeks sparkled a little in the bright ball-room light from the glitter in Serena's pale pink Vincent Longo lip gloss.

Which might have been cute in other circumstances but was definitely *not* cute right now.

Still, there was something amiss in their togetherness. Nate looked thin and depressed, and Serena looked distracted and spacier than usual. Blair satisfied herself with the notion that they were definitely not happy. Nate was probably always too stoned to pay attention to Serena in the way that she passive-aggressively demanded. And Serena probably forgot to call Nate all the time. He pretended not to like constant calling, but he secretly needed it the way only children always need to be reminded that they are the center of the universe. With a private, smug smile, Blair went back to the rack of Ghost dresses she'd been sorting through in a halfhearted attempt to find something original and irresistible to wear for Constance Billard's graduation ceremony, which was only two weeks away.

Exactly. Why waste energy on hating them when there were more important matters to attend to, like buying a dress?

Serena pulled off the hat she was wearing and tried on a black silk one with tiny faux pearls stitched all over it and a cropped black mesh just-over-the-eyes veil. She pursed her glossy lips at the mirror and decided she looked like Madonna in *Evita*, or some mobster's trophy wife. That was one of the things she loved about acting so much. She could bat her thick-lashed, deep blue eyes at the audience from behind a veil and suddenly she was a tragic figure badly in need of a little TLC or, at the very least, a stiff cocktail.

This particular hat was very dramatic, which was exactly the way she'd been feeling lately. Not depressed dramatic, or ecstatic dramatic, but behaving-in-a-way-that-wasn't-exactly-herself dramatic. She stole a sidelong glance at Blair, who was fervently flicking through a rack of dresses, refusing to even acknowledge Serena's presence. Serena exchanged the black hat for a hideous thick purple velvet headband with fake fruit and leaves sewn all over it. If only Blair would look her way, Serena knew she'd pee her pants with amusement. But Blair kept her back turned. Serena sighed. Only a week ago they'd been best friends again. Now this. She and Nate were together, and Blair wasn't speaking to them.

Hooking up in the bathroom at Isabel's party had been a total accident, and if Blair hadn't caught them, they probably would have left it at that. But it would have been just plain cruel to hook up in front of her and then not try to make it mean something. Though she and Nate had never actually discussed it, they both cared about Blair too much not to stay together so she wouldn't think it was just some random, horny hookup between two beautiful, self-centered people who couldn't control themselves.

Which, of course, it was.

Besides, it wasn't like being together was hard. They were both gorgeous, they loved each other—always had—and Serena's Fifth Avenue penthouse was only four blocks away from Nate's town house between Park and Lexington. Plus, all they really ever did was fool around because a) they'd known each other since they were toddlers, so there wasn't anything new to know, and b) even though Serena would have been happy to, they couldn't go all the way because Nate seemed to be having a problem lately. . . .

Oh? And what sort of "problem" might that be?

"Hey, Serena," Isabel called over from the Stella McCartney rack. "I heard you got nominated for senior speaker by Mr. Beckham."

Serena propped the purple-fruited headband back on its hook. "Really?" she responded with genuine amazement. Mr. Beckham was Constance Billard's film teacher. She had stopped taking film in ninth grade and hadn't even been at Constance the next two years. She'd been up at Hanover Academy, in New Hampshire—until she kind of missed the first few weeks of senior year and they wouldn't take her back. Why would Mr. Beckham, of all people, nominate her for senior speaker?

Good question.

"So, are you going to do it?" Isabel persisted.

Serena tried to imagine herself standing at the podium in Brick Church on Park Avenue, addressing her class, dressed in their pristine white dresses and white gloves. *Oh, the places you'll go. Our future's so bright, we're going to have to wear shades,* etc. She might have liked acting and modeling, but inspirational speaking wasn't exactly her thing. Surely one of her other classmates would be way more into it.

"Maybe," she replied, noncommittally.

You bitch, Blair thought, her ears aching from eavesdropping. Ever since the infamous bathtub incident at Isabel's party, Blair had been obsessively determined to surprise everyone by rising above Serena and Nate's stupid, hurtful behavior, making it look like she really couldn't give a damn, and end the school year as the girl everyone most admired.

Not that she wasn't already the girl everyone most admired. She'd always had the best clothes, best bags, best fingernails, coolest hair, and by far the best shoes. But this time she wanted to be admired for her courage, independence, and intelligence. And being senior speaker at graduation was definitely part of that package. Right now Vanessa Abrams,

Blair's unlikely, shaven-headed, black-wearing roommate, was back at Constance nominating Blair for senior speaker. But as usual, that sneaky bitch Serena had to go and fucking copy her.

The tricky part of it was, no one actually campaigned to be senior speaker. And usually there wasn't even a vote, because usually only one person got nominated. Becoming senior speaker was one of those things that just *happened*— another mysterious Constance Billard tradition that no one ever quite understood. Things were bound to get a little interesting now that two girls were about to be nominated.

Especially these two.

Serena understood instantly that Blair would think that she actually wanted to be senior speaker, which was totally not the case. But how could she defend herself when Blair wouldn't even look at her? Unable to resist, she pointed at the goth-wears-white Morgane Le Fay dress in Blair's hands. "Oh my God, that would look so amazing on Vanessa. That's who it's for, right?" she asked with a bright smile.

Oh, so you think it's okay to talk to me? Blair thought. *Wrong.* Unable to muster a succinct spoken reply, Blair shrugged and carried the dress over to the makeshift register set up on a banquet table near the door, paying for it with one of her three platinum credit cards, which were paid off by her mother's accountant, Ralph.

This isn't going to be easy, Serena thought with a theatrical sigh. "I'm not in the mood to buy anything anyway," she added out loud and glanced around for Nate. Fighting with Blair was always so exhausting. Especially when it involved being madly in love with Nate Archibald.

Or at least, pretending to be.

he's come undone

Nate was outside the hotel with the trunk show security guard, smoking a hand-rolled pot-mixed-with-tobacco cigarette. The sun beat down on Fifth Avenue and Sixty-first Street, and with the masses of European tourists and clouds of bus exhaust, it felt more like late August than the last week in May.

"Beautiful day," the security guard, whose gold plastic name tag read DARWIN, remarked. He was huge and bald and probably moonlighted as a nightclub bouncer. He squeezed his eyes shut to ward off the bright, late-morning sun. "Summer is right around the corner."

Nate pressed his knuckles into his closed eyelids to keep the tears from streaming down his cheeks. He could blame it on the sun, or he could blame it on being dragged along to a trunk show with a girl, but the truth was that lately he'd been crying a lot. It was the end of their senior year, and he was with Serena, the girl he'd loved forever—kind of. It was like he was finally tasting the meal he'd been looking at under glass all those years. He wanted to savor it, but everyone else was eating so quickly, there wasn't time. And there was also this nagging feeling that he'd ordered the wrong thing.

Wait, doesn't he mean the wrong girl?

"Should I be worried about one of your girlfriends in

there stealing something?" Darwin asked. He pulled a silvery blue cell phone out of his pants pocket, scrolled through a few text messages on the screen, then stuffed the phone back in his pocket. He didn't seem too worried. Then again, why would someone with biceps that large get nervous about a few devious teenage girls?

Blair had been known to shoplift, but not in front of her friends. Nate had never heard about Serena shoplifting, but she had a naughty streak. She would do it out of sheer boredom. He shrugged. "Probably."

Just then the hotel porter opened the door and Blair skipped down the red-carpeted stairs, brushing past Nate with her pointed foxlike chin in the air and a white shopping bag with white tissue paper sticking out of it swinging back and forth from her hand.

"She's *cute*," Darwin whistled.

"Uh-huh," Nate grunted, as if checking Blair out for the first time. Her silky, dark hair had grown into a very French-looking short and sexy bob that suited her finely featured face and hot little body. Oh, she was cute all right.

And she was no longer his.

"Want me to stop her? Check her bags?" Darwin offered.

Nate puffed on his joint, considering how Blair would react if Darwin called her over. The thought made him smile wistfully, and as he watched Blair disappear down the crowded block, fresh tears began to spill down his cheeks. Bitchy and stubborn and selfish and neurotic, Blair was the epitome of high maintenance, but no matter how many times he'd fucked up, she'd always taken him back. It usually started with a sidelong glance or an irate phone call, and then he'd show up at her door and they'd kiss and make up. But Blair wasn't sending him any if-you're-really-nice-to-me-I'll-consider-it vibes. It seemed he'd fucked up for the last time. Besides, he was with Serena now, everybody's dream girl.

Everybody including him?

The porter opened the door again, and Serena glided out of the hotel sporting a mint green linen Les Best tennis visor. With her pale golden hair cascading down from beneath the visor, her long, tanned, athletic-even-though-she-got-no-exercise-except-for-gym-class legs, and radiant smile, she looked like an advertisement for the type of haute couture tennis clothes that were way too gorgeous to actually sweat in.

"Taxi back to school?" she asked Nate with a sly wink. She might have been too tired to walk, but she wasn't too tired to fool around in the back of a taxi.

Who could ever be too tired for that?

Then she noticed the tears. "Poor baby," she crooned, reaching out to dab at Nate's cheeks with her thumb. The crying had started a few days ago, and at first it had been sort of alarming. What was a handsome stoner stud like Nate doing *crying*? But then she'd grown to think of it as sexy and extremely touching. Who knew Nate had such a sweet, gooey center?

Darwin took a step forward. He wasn't about to let this blond bombshell get away as quickly as the hot brunette had. "You got a receipt for that hat, miss?"

Serena reached up to touch the linen visor like she'd forgotten she was wearing it. She bit her luxuriously full, cherry-ChapSticked lips. "Oops." Her dark blue eyes flashed, challenging Darwin to arrest her. "I'm friends with the designer," she declared.

Darwin grinned—yet another guy to fall under her spell. "Aw, that's okay," he replied bashfully. "I guess I just wanted an excuse to talk to you."

Nate realized suddenly that he ought to have been jealous. He took Serena's dry, warm hand in his damp, tear-streaked one. "Come on," he urged, trying to sound manly and firm despite the quaver in his voice.

"God, I love it when you fight for me," Serena murmured. She leaned her head against his shoulder and kissed his right ear. He put his arm around her waist, encouraged by the strong curve of her hip. They tripped down the steps, barely resisting the urge to tear each other's clothes off right there in front of the hundreds of fanny-pack-toting tourists mobbing the Brooks Brothers flagship store across the street. Their getting together might have been a total accident, but they were still two beautiful, irresistibly kissable people—why not take every possible opportunity to fool around?

Exactly.

"Lucky guy." Darwin whistled as he headed back inside to hit on Rain or Kati or whichever cute Constance girl had the most stuff in her bag.

Nate fought back another rush of tears. He was into Yale. The most beautiful girl in the universe, whom he'd known forever, was practically begging him to do it with him in a taxi on the way back to school. He *was* insanely lucky.

So why couldn't he stop the tears from falling?

v's first love note of the day

To: vabrams@constancebillard.edu
From: aaron.rose@bronxdale.edu
Subject: idea of the day

Okay I know I just kissed you good-bye
like an hour ago, but I had an awesome
idea on the way up to school—man that's a
long-ass subway ride! Anyway, what if we
just get done with our finals and skip
graduation because a) it's going to be
boring, b) our parents couldn't care less,
and c) you said yourself you're not really
a white-dress kind of gal. We could take
off in the Saab, drive to the Grand
Canyon, watch the sun set, eat some one
hundred percent organic wild mushrooms,
and dance naked with the coyotes out under
the stars. I want to spend the summer
exploring the country and holding you in
the glorious moonlight. Damn, there's the

bell. Anyway, think about it. You're my
girl.

Love you,
A

d is mr. popularity

"So, it looks like it's unanimous. Daniel Humphrey, you're our graduation speaker this year," announced Dan's Riverside Prep senior homeroom teacher, Mr. Cohen, head of the history department, who insisted the boys call him Larry.

"Huh?" Dan looked up from the poem he was scribbling in his ever-present black-leather-bound book. The poem was called "my highway" and was all about the incredible journey Dan was about to embark on. Since there was nothing keeping him in the city, he'd decided to leave early for Evergreen College, where he was going in the fall. He'd already applied for a summer job there through the college's employment office Web site. And right after graduation, he was going to drive all the way there to Olympia, Washington. If he ever got a car, or even learned how to drive.

Oops.

Dan had decided to model himself after Jack Kerouac when he was writing *On the Road*. On his journey west, he'd hook up with the most gorgeous local girls in every town, try exotic new food and drink, like peyote and two-hundred-proof tequila, and make detours to bizarre local attractions, like caves with hundred-foot-long stalactites and bleeding rocks, or a cow with quintuplets. He'd already been published in the *New Yorker* at the impressive age of seventeen and had a brief stint as the lead singer for the popular rock band the Raves, but when he arrived in Washington State, all the hell the way across the country, he'd have a new degree from the College of Life.

Bucking girls and shucking corn,
Rodeo bullhorns, Stetsoned longhorns, a Kansas cyclone.
A Nebraskan girl leaves her lipstick on the dash—
She salts my beef, stirs my gumbo, spits out my pit.

Uh-oh. Sounds like he was a rock star for one day too many.

"The class voted for you and you alone," Larry explained. "You should feel extremely honored."

Dan was mystified. He pushed his chair back, crossed his grubby blue Pumas one over the other, and shoved his hands into the pockets of his worn-in khaki-colored cords. "But I didn't even nominate myself," he blurted out.

Way to make it obvious that you have no friends.

Snickers erupted throughout the room.

"It's like, you're a celebrity, man, and we want you to represent us," Chuck Bass explained in a mock stoner voice. Chuck's pet snow monkey, Sweetie, was curled up in a fuzzy white ball in Chuck's lap, asleep, wearing his favorite tight, cantaloupe-colored T-shirt with a bright pink *S* on the back of it. Everyone, even the teachers, had gotten so used to the monkey, they didn't bat an eye, but Sweetie still gave Dan the creeps.

"We figured it'd be easy for you, since you're writing all the time anyway," Chuck continued sarcastically. More snickers.

Dan tipped his chair back. "Wait. Let me get this straight. *You* nominated me?"

Chuck flipped up the collar on his bright purple short-sleeved Lacoste shirt. "It's like Larry said. It was unanimous."

Dan's hands began to sweat. Senior speaker was an honor,

but he felt like he'd gotten it by default. He certainly wasn't the most popular guy in the class. He'd spent his entire senior year either trying to become famous or hanging out with his former best friend and girlfriend, Vanessa, in Williamsburg, Brooklyn. He guessed all the other guys in his class were going to be too busy partying or trying not to fail their finals to bother writing a graduation speech.

"Just keep it light. And remember, everyone just wants that diploma in his hands, so keep it short, too," Larry advised, pulling on his lame dirty blond goatee like the wannabe teenage boy he so totally wasn't.

"Okay," Dan responded dubiously. It appeared he had no choice in the matter.

Chuck tapped him on the shoulder. "So guess what? That dykey girlfriend of yours? I heard she's gonna be single again. Her 'better half' is totally moving out."

Meaning Vanessa or Aaron? Dan wasn't even sure anymore who Vanessa was living with. All he knew was it wasn't him. His perspiration-soaked hands began to shake with a mixture of confusion and happiness. Maybe Vanessa had broken up with Aaron. But they were so in love. They even had matching haircuts. He scribbled a series of check marks across the top of the page he'd been writing on. Vanessa broke up with Aaron!?

"So I take it you're accepting the nomination," Larry persisted, tapping his pencil annoyingly against his wooden teacher desk. "All in favor say, 'Yeah!'"

"Dude!" the class of boys responded in unison, perpetuating the not-so-funny tradition that had started on the first day of senior year. Dan blanched as they began to whoop and shriek in a completely unnecessary display of fake enthusiasm. "Go, Dan!"

The minute the bell rang, Dan called Vanessa to tell her how sorry he was.

Yeah, right.

"Talk about misinformation!" Vanessa ranted. "Where do people get this shit? So, how are you anyway?" she asked, sounding kind of glad to hear from him.

"I was just voted senior speaker," Dan admitted, like he'd been campaigning for it for weeks. Secretly, he was dying inside that Vanessa and Aaron were still together, but he wasn't about to let her know that.

"Senior speaker? What the fuck!" Vanessa responded. "Wait, is that a good thing?"

"I guess."

"Look, I have photo lab now, but do you want to come over later or something?"

Dan pressed his cell phone against his ear until it began to hurt. A group of freshmen boys almost sent him toppling down the stairs in their rush to lunch. All of a sudden he realized just how lonely he'd been. Was it really possible that he and Vanessa could be friends again, just like that, with one phone call?

And if they could be friends again, there was always the chance they could be more.

"Will Aaron be there?" he asked cautiously as he wandered down the fourth-floor hallway toward English class. A random, lint-covered rubber band was in his pocket. He pulled his scraggly, light brown hair into a stubby ponytail and then pulled it out again, dropping the rubber band on the floor. His dad, Rufus, was Mr. Ponytail Freak, not him.

"Aaron has band practice," Vanessa told him casually. "Not that you couldn't come over even if he were here."

Hello, threesome?!

Dan felt like a window was swinging open and a cool breeze was sweeping his face. "I'm supposed to go to this stupid AP history cram session for our final next week, but I could skip it."

Chuck Bass's monkey scampered past him down the hall with a half-eaten bag of Smart Puffs in his mouth. Chuck was too busy dabbing Aveda pomade into his freshly highlighted hair in front of the full-length mirror he'd installed inside his locker to even notice.

"Okay, I'm in photo lab now. As usual, everyone else cut except me. They're all probably at some stupid sample sale or something. Shopping for their stupid white wedding—I mean, graduation gowns or whatever. *Fuck!*" Vanessa exclaimed, sounding like she'd stumbled into something. "It's dark in here."

Dan's ear was sweating now. "I wish I were there," he blurted out, unable to stop himself.

"Me too," Vanessa responded eagerly. "Seriously."

Wait, was she *flirting* with him?

"So maybe I will come over later," he ventured. "Dad and Jenny are away anyway, so I don't have to be home at any particular time."

Is that so?

"Cool." Vanessa sounded distracted now. "Look, I'm gonna do something dumb like drink fixer instead of my tea if I don't hang up now. I'll see you later, okay?"

Dan could hardly wait. "Yeah, okay." He hung up. Down the hall Sweetie was peeing on the marble floor in front of the door to the history department offices. Dan grinned at him.

Good boy.

s has rendered party school totally useless

"So just drink some coffee and read poetry quietly to yourself, okay, Dad?" Jenny Humphrey pleaded with her uncooperative father, Rufus, as they stood in front of the dapper wrought-iron gates of Hanover Academy, just outside the quaint and lovely town of Hanover, New Hampshire. After appearing semiclothed on the Internet and in the pages of various fashion magazines, and colluding with post-college-age rock stars in their suite at the Plaza Hotel, Jenny had been given an ultimatum by Mrs. McLean, headmistress of Constance Billard. She had to stop making headlines and finish up her freshman year at Constance behaving like the demure school girl she was supposed to be or she'd have to find some other school to attend in the fall. Jenny had taken this as a challenge and wound up spending an entire weekend with the Raves in the lead guitarist's Bedford Street town house. She'd even recorded a song with them! The following Monday, Mrs. McLean and everyone else in the city had read all about it in the gossip columns.

Say good-bye to Constance Billard and hello to . . . *boarding school*!

Now it was the following Monday and Jenny had taken the day off from school to look at Hanover, the famously wild and crazy boarding school of her dreams. Hanover was where party girl extraordinaire Serena van der Woodsen had gone for two years before getting kicked out last October, and Jenny imagined that Serena had never been replaced. Well, here *she* was to replace her. She was going to bring Hanover to new heights of infamy, and if, for some reason—which was hard to imagine—Hanover didn't appeal to her, or worse, didn't accept her, she would also visit the Croton School. Croton was only an hour and a half away from the city, in Croton Falls, New York, and according to all the prep school guidebooks Jenny had been reading, it was almost as wild as Hanover.

"I might get a haircut, too," Rufus replied, sounding chipper. His wiry salt-and-pepper hair was pulled back into a straggly ponytail held by a rainbow-colored twist-tie that had come on a bag of flaxseed bagels from the Whole Foods near their Upper West Side apartment building. To go with his fancy hairstyle, Rufus was wearing a red-and-white checked Western-style snap-up-the-front short-sleeved shirt, heavy brown canvas Carhartt work shorts, and scuffed beige suede Birkenstock clogs with black wool socks.

Nothing like the country to bring out one's sense of fashion.

"Oh. Good." Jenny tried not to get too excited. The last time Rufus had gotten his hair cut—sometime around her thirteenth birthday—he had gone to a Lower East Side salon popular with drag queens and gotten bangs with purple streaks in them. "So, I'll just go on my tour and meet you at that place in town," she added, referring to the bookstore café they'd passed on the way through the town of Hanover. The campus was a mile-and-a-half walk from town along a nice tree-lined path. It would be reassuring to have that distance between herself and Rufus, in case he decided to start a political movement or something equally insane out of sheer anxiety at having to leave the city.

"You got it!" Rufus pecked her on the cheek with his grizzly mouth before striding down the path with exaggerated jauntiness. "Don't do anything I wouldn't do!" he called out behind him.

As if there were anything he wouldn't do.

Jenny tugged on the pretty jade green cap-sleeved blouse she'd bought at Scoop in Soho on Saturday. It was Japanese and had little dragonflies stenciled all over it. She'd buttoned it up all the way to the collar, but now that her dad was on his way, she unbuttoned the top two buttons, revealing her most surprising assets—her 34 double-Ds.

No reason the boys at Hanover shouldn't know what they were in for.

She extracted her laminated campus map from her bought-on-the-street-outside-of-Bloomingdales-but-looked-just-like-Serena's imitation Louis Vuitton Calla Lily bag. The school's ivy-covered old brick buildings were right out of an Abercrombie & Fitch catalog, but Jenny was disappointed not to see any gorgeous, half-naked, sun-dappled boys playing Frisbee out on the lawns. Riley, the girls' dormitory where she'd arranged to meet her host, was on the other side of the parking lot, perched on top of a grassy hillock. It was a gorgeous summer day, and the air smelled like fresh-cut grass.

"I already love it here," Jenny whispered, her skin tingling with excitement. Her whole life was about to change. No more uniforms. No more bitchy, cliquey girls who would spend hours dissecting a girl's choice of mauve lip gloss over pink. No more being known only for her excellent calligraphy, her overhyped Internet scandal, or her supposedly pornographic photo shoots. No more rumors, no more scandal.

Well, maybe that was taking it a little too far. There was nothing wrong with a little scandal. It was just that at a boarding school like Hanover, the bar for scandal would be considerably higher.

Jenny's host, Fiona Castagnoli, was waiting for her outside the door to Riley. Fiona looked like a forty-five-year-old soccer mom—short and pudgy, in a coral-pink-and-white striped J.Crew oxford shirt tucked into stone-colored L.L. Bean Bermuda shorts. Her white socks were folded neatly at the ankle, and her white-on-white Reebok sneakers were brand-spanking-new. "Jennifer?" she asked eagerly, her supercurly, tight auburn ponytail bouncing between her shoulder blades. "We have to hurry. I'm taking you to study hall and we're already five minutes late!"

Fiona was lugging a lime green Lands' End backpack with every book she owned in it. Jenny blinked at her. When she'd thought about coming to visit Hanover, she'd imagined hanging out in a dorm room with chic skinny blond girls, drinking vodka gimlets and flirting with boys smoking pipes, their school neckties flopping loosely against their tanned bare chests. "If you have lots of work to do I could, like, hang out here and wait for you," she offered.

"Oh, could you?" Fiona cried. She seemed immensely relieved. "You see, it's finals week next week, and I have forty-seven Spanish irregulars to study and thirteen proofs to do for geometry."

Jenny peered inside the open door. A few girls lounged in leather armchairs in the crystal-chandeliered common room reading magazines and listening to their iPod minis. Jenny recognized a red-and-white rose-patterned Marc Jacobs top on one of them. And one girl was wearing the pair of gold Belle by Sigerson Morrison flats she'd coveted all spring but had never saved up enough to buy. They looked exactly like the types of girls she would have wanted to be friends with. All that was missing were the boys with the pipes and the vodka.

"I'll stay here," she told Fiona firmly.

"Okay." Fiona hitched her ugly green backpack up on her shoulder. "I'll come back and get you in, like, an hour and ten. We can get bagels in the café and I'll show you my room."

Whoa, sounds like a party.

Jenny was already sure she was never going to see Fiona again because Fiona was going to get so caught up in her irregular verbs or whatever, she'd forget all about how she'd left Jenny with the coolest, worst-behaved girls at Hanover. She pulled a tube of Chanel Stroppy lip gloss out of her bag and smeared some on. Then she stepped inside the common room. "Hi," she announced shyly. "I'm Jennifer. I'm visiting from the city? I go to Constance Billard—you know, where Serena van der Woodsen went?" She knew it was lame to mention Serena right away, but she wanted these girls to know that she was cool, that she was one of them.

One girl with short black hair and beautifully painted Chanel Vamp toenails glanced her way but then looked quickly away again. Other than that, no one seemed to hear what she'd said. The wood paneling in the common room gave off an amber glow, and the oriental carpet beneath Jenny's feet was in perfect condition. She felt like she was in the den of some old mansion rather than in a school.

"So, I hear Hanover can get pretty crazy sometimes. At least, that's what Serena told me," Jenny babbled on, still standing in the doorway like an idiot. She wanted to make it very clear that she didn't just know *of* Serena. They were pals.

"Shush," whispered a beautiful blond girl with legs so long and so tan, they looked fake. "You're going to get us in trouble."

Hello? Since when were Hanover girls worried about getting into trouble?

"Sorry," Jenny muttered meekly. She sat down in an empty leather chair, wincing at the noisy farting sound it made when her bare legs rubbed against it. She placed her faux Louis Vuitton bag primly on her lap, wishing she'd at least thought to bring a book. Out of the corner of her eye, she caught the girl with short black hair checking her out once more. Jenny pulled an old receipt from Duane Reade out of the side pocket of her bag and then hunted for the stubby Hello Kitty pencil she'd had since fifth grade.

What's the deal? I thought Hanover was supposed to be totally WILD, she scribbled on the back of the receipt. Then she folded up the receipt and daringly tossed it in the short-haired girl's lap. Less than a minute later the receipt came back with blue pen all over it. *Well, basically, the little episode with your friend Serena (who used to be my neighbor here in Riley—when she was actually around) ruined everything. After getting rid of her, they instituted the disciplinary code, which basically says that if you tell on your friends, you get privileges. There's so much incentive to tell on your friends that no one ever does anything worth talking about anymore. This place is totally dry, quiet, and B.O.R.I.N.G!!! I'm a senior, though, so I'm outta here— YAY!*

Jenny looked up from the note and studied the other girls in the room more carefully. One of the iPod listeners was muttering to herself, and Jenny realized she wasn't listening to the latest downloads but rather memorizing Spanish conjugations. A petite Asian girl with thick pigtails who Jenny had thought was reading a fashion magazine was actually completely engrossed in *Science Digest.*

Uh-oh.

I probably wouldn't get in anyway, Jenny scribbled back. She tossed the note to the girl, then stood up. Applications for boarding school were supposed to have been done in the fall, so she was pushing it timewise wherever she decided to go, never mind who would have her. But surely there were other schools that weren't quite as strict as Hanover clearly was now.

She went outside and wound her way back to the school gates, wishing that she hadn't sent her father away in such a hurry. Heading down the path toward town she came upon a blond boy in a red Ralph Lauren baseball cap, a white V-neck T-shirt, and floppy aqua-colored J.Crew linen pants, smoking a Marlboro as he shuffled slowly back toward campus. He was completely adorable.

Jenny smiled shyly at him as he approached, mustering up the courage to ask him if Hanover was really as bad as that short-haired girl back in Riley had made it out to be.

"You're not going to tell on me, are you?" the boy demanded, glaring at her with more hostility than anyone deserves.

"N-no," Jenny stammered. Was everyone at Hanover totally paranoid?

"Right," he sneered back, still glaring as he shuffled away.

When she arrived at the coffee shop, her dad was behind the counter whipping up a soy milk chai latte, even though he and Dan had spent an hour one day lecturing Jenny on how chai was just some made-up Starbucks bullshit and how the only real hot drink on the planet was Folgers instant coffee. "The air is so fine, I was thinking I might move up here. They even offered me a job here in the café," he crowed, beaming at her. "Dan's off to Evergreen in the fall anyway. We'll sublet our place—make a fortune!"

"Sorry, Dad, but I don't think so," Jenny sighed. "I mean, I don't think I want to go here."

Rufus carried the paper cup of frothy hot liquid around the counter and handed it to Jenny. "You mean you want to stay home with me?" he asked, his bushy salt-and-pepper eyebrows arched hopefully.

Jenny smelled the drink, made a face, and then handed it back. "No. I just have to keep looking. Croton's on the way home anyway."

Rufus winked at the big-hipped, hemp-dress-wearing, frizzy-haired woman coming out of the kitchen with a tray of buckwheat scones in her hands. He sighed. "You sure?"

From what Jenny could remember, the prep school guidebook she'd read from cover to cover in the corner by the window upstairs at the Broadway Barnes & Noble had listed

Croton Academy in Croton Falls second on the list of party schools, right after Hanover. Croton was supposed to be full of kids who'd been kicked out of their New York City private schools for bad behavior. Obviously the book hadn't been updated recently if it still listed Hanover as the number one party school, but maybe what it said about Croton was still true.

"Come on, let's *go*." Jenny tugged on the pocket of her father's Carhartt shorts, all excited about Croton now.

It sounded way cooler than Hanover. And hopefully it had no disciplinary code.

Professor Pierre Papadametriou
English Dept., The Evergreen State College
2700 Evergreen Parkway NW
Olympia, WA 98505

Daniel Humphrey
815 West End Avenue, Apt. 8D
New York, NY 10024

Dear Mr. Daniel Humphrey,
I saw your query in Seeking Paid Summer Internship on college employment site. I am poetry and biology professor at college and I seek summer intern. You live in my house. I have two dogs and a son. My wife left for Greece. Son is fisherman. Dogs live outside. You work on my very interesting book with me. I feed you good Greek food! Tell me when you come and I will fix hammock in attic. Must go feed dogs. They love my moussaka!

Please write back soon.
Pierre

d and v have déjà vu . . . all over again

"Wow. Your place looks really . . . *lavender*," Dan remarked when Vanessa let him in. When he'd lived there the walls of the small, nondescript apartment had been plain, peeling, and white, and there'd been black Halloween sheets hanging in the windows in place of curtains. Now the walls were painted a delicate light lavender with celery green trim, and black-and-white chintz curtains hung from real curtain rods in the windows. There were a nice Danish modern wooden table and chairs in the living room and a cool, modern gray sofa. The place looked like it had been decorated by a real decorator.

Vanessa blushed, which was weird for her. Since when did she blush? "Blair kind of spruced it up a little. You like?"

Dan was sweaty from the subway ride, and because he'd run all the way from the L stop, thirteen blocks away. He traced a sticky finger over the freshly painted wall, his heart beating fast. "It's different, I guess," he responded nervously. Vanessa was checking him out in that unabashed, direct way of hers, making him sweat even harder.

When Vanessa had gotten home from school, there'd been a little white box waiting for her on the kitchen counter. She'd opened it to find a silver ring in the shape of two hands holding hearts that were welded together. Inside the ring was the inscription FOREVER AND ALWAYS. LOVE, A. Except for a brief dalliance with a lip ring, Vanessa rarely wore jewelry, and this type of friendship/love ring was so corny it made her laugh. She'd certainly never have considered wearing it, no matter who had given it to her. She'd dropped the ring back inside the box and tucked it into the silverware drawer. It was possible Aaron had given her the ring as a joke, but then why would he have bothered to have it inscribed? Even when they were going out, Dan would never have given her such a sappy gift. Come to think of it, he'd never asked her to camp out under the stars with him, either. Vanessa was a running-water-and-flushing-toilets sort of girl. She hated the sun, and the outdoors, with its spiders, ants, bees, and mosquitoes, creeped her out. Of course, Aaron meant well. It was the thought that counted and all that. But she and he would have to talk—something they hadn't really done much of since they'd hooked up. Despite Aaron pouring on the love notes, giving her gifts, and sleeping over all the time, their relationship had been purely physical thus far.

Not that she minded. There was something about the stress of finals and graduation and turning a new page in life that was secretly freaking Vanessa out. She simply wasn't herself. Or maybe living in an apartment with lavender walls with a girl who owned one hundred seventeen pairs of shoes, including thirty-four pairs of Manolo Blahniks, had turned her into someone else. Formerly a loner, Vanessa could no longer bear to be alone, and she'd found that the best way to keep her mind off the future was to drink a little vodka and then fool around.

She's only just discovered this?

"You look pale," Vanessa told Dan. Then she took a step toward him, wrapped her arms around his neck, and kissed him on the cheek. She squeezed her eyes shut and inhaled his cute, musty Dan scent. "Pale, but really good."

Vanessa was wearing a black ribbed tank top and no bra.

Her head was freshly shaved, but she'd allowed the dark hair around her face to grow half an inch or so, softening her broad white forehead and big brown eyes. And she'd given up on her lip ring.

Which was a good thing.

She was also wearing a flippy black miniskirt that she never would have considered before Blair Waldorf moved in. But she'd paired the miniskirt with black-and-white argyle kneesocks and her ever-present Doc Martens, making it very clear that, despite her roommate's influence, she wasn't about to buy a pair of snakeskin Manolo Blahnik stilettos anytime soon, even if they came in black.

The smooth slope of her pale upper arms, the mocking curve of her red lips, and the defiant glow in her big brown eyes made Dan wonder how he'd ever functioned without her. He resisted the urge to whip out his leather-bound notebook and scribble down a poem. Instead he pulled a Camel out of the pack and stuck it between his lips without lighting it. "So, you want to take a walk? Get some coffee or something?" he ventured, trying to sound vaguely normal.

Vanessa shrugged her shoulders without moving away from him. "I'm having a major déjà vu," she confessed with a bemused smile. Wasn't this how they'd gotten together again the last time? He'd come over and then they'd basically ripped each other's clothes off.

"Me too," he admitted, secretly hoping that history would repeat itself.

"Blair and I just discovered a door to the roof of the building. All this time I thought it was padlocked, but the lock is totally broken. It's pretty cool up there—want to check it out?"

So was Vanessa into sunbathing now too? "Sure," Dan agreed.

To his surprise, she collected a quart of Absolut and a bottle of tonic water from the fridge, tucking them into a paper bag with two plastic Scooby-Doo glasses, which she filled with ice. "I've kind of developed a taste for this stuff," she admitted with a wicked grin.

Dan stared at her in amazement, his whole body trembling with anticipation. Vanessa never could hold her liquor; neither could he.

He followed her out of the apartment, down the dirty, cement-floored hall, and up the building's cruddy stairs, which were painted black and smelled of turpentine. Two flights up, Vanessa pushed open a black metal door marked DO NOT ENTER and stepped out into the bright hot light of the rooftop. Suddenly the city was all around them, and the Williamsburg Bridge seemed close enough to touch. Off to the right, the East River looked glassy and cool as a sailing yacht glided past a barge pulling a load of Porta Johns, its white sails luffing in the thick afternoon air. To their left was the sugar factory, billowing smoke out of great smokestacks and adding to the smog. Across the bridge, Manhattan loomed large and full of promises. A born Manhattanite, Dan could never get over the feeling when he was in Brooklyn that something exciting was going on across the water, and that he was missing out.

"Over here," Vanessa called over the roar of interborough traffic. She ducked under a metal beam supporting the giant wooden water tower that dominated the roof. "We're totally protected from the sun and rain under here. And see, the condensation from the water tower even keeps the air kind of cool."

Dan went over and ducked under the water tower. A black futon was spread out on the ground, complete with an assortment of black fake fur throw pillows. Vanessa seemed to have her own outdoor love den.

"You and Aaron must spend a lot of time up here," he commented awkwardly.

She sat down on the futon and began pouring vodka into

the plastic Scooby-Doo glasses. "Actually, I promised Blair not to hog it. We only just discovered it on Saturday, and yesterday it was raining, so actually Aaron's never even been up here."

Meaning she and Aaron had never done it up there, which kind of made Dan feel better about sitting down on the futon. Vanessa handed him a vodka tonic. "Sorry, no limes."

He sat down and lit a cigarette. A helicopter motored loudly by. He had to admit, this was kind of a cool place to be.

"So, graduation speaker, huh? I was even thinking about maybe skipping my graduation." Vanessa clicked her glass against his and then took a big, long sip. "To us."

Dan squinted at her as he drank, holding the plastic glass with his cigarette hand, his pale face to the sun. There was something different about Vanessa this time. Something lazy and dangerous and sexy.

Cobra curled on hot cement, his mind began writing furiously, because it couldn't help itself.

Vanessa grinned, returning his intense stare with a self-conscious chuckle. "I don't know why I'm doing this but . . ." she began. Then she put down her glass, leaned slowly toward him, and shoved her tongue down his throat.

Whoa!

Dan's dreamy brown eyes grew huge. He wondered if maybe Vanessa had been drinking all day and had somehow confused him with Aaron. Or maybe he and Aaron had gotten caught in some sort of mind-melt-time-warp-space-time-continuum-body-swapping ordeal straight out of the type of bad comic book he used to read when he was nine, and he really *was* Aaron. Nevertheless, it was sheer ecstasy kissing Vanessa again, and sheer agony to even think of pulling away. But after a few minutes, he forced himself to do it. "Um, can I just ask you—what are we doing?"

Vanessa grabbed the hem of his faded red Stussy T-shirt and lifted it up, peeking at his pale, flat stomach. "Don't you sometimes wonder what the big deal is?" she asked, as if that were answer enough.

Dan didn't say anything. Vanessa seemed to be going through some sort of experimental period, and he wasn't about to get in the way, especially since it seemed to involve wanting to take his shirt off. And his pants. Even his socks seemed to be getting in the way of her need to express herself. And just so she wouldn't feel left out, he helped her off with her clothes, too. Before long they were kneeling on the futon beneath the water tower, naked.

Talk about déjà vu!

you can take the girl out of 212, but you can't take the 212 out of the girl

"Do you have anything that isn't . . . *shiny*?" Blair Waldorf demanded as she fingered the dresses on the circular rack in the back of Isn't She Lovely, a tiny Williamsburg bridal and special-occasion-dresses boutique a block away from the apartment she shared with Vanessa. She walked by the boutique every day on her way to and from the coffee shop where a car service town car picked her up in the morning after she bought her large latte with an extra shot of espresso and dropped her off after school. Today she'd wandered inside, thinking it might be cool to buy a graduation dress in a place so completely off the map that no other girl in the senior class at Constance Billard could possibly have the same one she did. The problem was, with no designer label to show their merit, she wasn't sure if the dresses were ugly in a cool way or just plain ugly.

"This one is very popular for confirmations," the overly perfumed saleslady told her in heavily accented English. She held up a dazzling white, rhinestone-encrusted, polyester-lace-bodiced sundress with a pleated skirt that was so stiff and shiny, it looked like it had been laminated.

Blair glanced in one of the many mirrors all over the store and glared at the haughty brunette in a short light-blue-and-white seersucker Constance Billard uniform skirt and neat white-collared, baby pink polo shirt staring back at her, furious with herself all of a sudden. Who was she kidding, pretending not to need a graduation dress that was made to order by Oscar de la Renta or Chanel? She hitched her nude pink Fendi purse up on her shoulder and slid her tortoiseshell Parsol sunglasses up on her nose, tempted to buy the hideous dress the saleslady had just shown her and bring it home to Vanessa as a joke, pretending she was going to wear it to graduation. But the thought of spending money on anything so hideous, even in jest, made her even more furious. When had her life become so *base*?

Maybe when she decided to ditch Manhattan and become a Brooklyn hipster?

Usually Blair couldn't leave a store without buying at least one thing, but usually the stores she went into were stocked with irresistibles. As far as Blair was concerned, Isn't She Lovely should have been named Isn't She Ugly.

Across the litter-strewn expanse of Broadway from Vanessa's crumbling gray, five-story walk-up apartment building, a cluster of people stood looking up, their mouths agape.

Hmm, wonder why?

Oblivious and not at all curious about anything the locals might find interesting, Blair hurried across the street, mounted the crumbling cement stoop, and unlocked the building's graffitied front door. She held her breath as she climbed the steps up to Vanessa's second-story apartment. The building was practically sitting on top of a sugar factory, and the air around it was as sweet and heavy as syrup-logged French toast—mixed with a twinge of stray cat pee.

Yum.

"Foul," Blair muttered aloud while still trying to hold her breath. How she longed for the immaculate putty-colored marble lobby of the Seventy-second Street full-service, white-glove, luxury apartment building where she'd lived until now.

Oh, how she missed the sweep of the doorman's hunter green wool cape as he opened the door to her cab and helped her with her bags, shielding her from the rain with his enormous black umbrella. How she yearned for the hum of the burgundy velvet-upholstered-elevator as it whisked her up to the penthouse.

The black-painted door to the apartment was standing open, shedding little chips of old black paint onto the dusty cement floor of the hallway. "Honey, I'm home!" Blair called out tentatively as she stepped inside the apartment that she'd gladly redecorated only a few weeks before in shades of lavender, dove gray, and celery. The small, low-ceilinged one-bedroom looked so much prettier than it had when she'd moved in, especially without those revolting black sheets in the windows. She and Vanessa had even bonded—they really had. And it was fun to live somewhere so different from the place where she'd grown up. Really, it was. But she was still a little homesick. After all, Isn't She Lovely was hardly a replacement for Barneys.

"Oh, *yeah*. Oh, *yeah*. Oh, *yes*!" a boy's voice, hoarse with ecstasy, echoed down the back stairway and into the apartment.

Ew.

Blair's lips curled into a grimace. Vanessa and Aaron were at it again, up on the roof. Not that they hadn't spent the entire night last night moaning and howling like wild dogs. Blair's stomach turned and she poured herself a glass of water from the Brita filter she'd bought because she didn't trust the water in Brooklyn. Since breaking up with Nate, she hadn't once made herself sick—that would be the ultimate sign of weakness, and she was no longer weak—but the image of Vanessa and Aaron, their shaved heads locked and their pale bodies thrashing up on the roof in broad daylight, was too similar to the image of Serena and Nate thrashing around in Isabel Coates's pool house bathtub. It was enough to make her want to violently hurl the mango smoothie she'd drunk three hours ago.

Gulping her glass of water, she gripped the cracked white Formica countertop to steady herself. On the ancient electric stove was a pot of stale water with two cold, gray-pink tofu dogs lolling inside—leftovers from her stepbrother Aaron's disgusting breakfast, or lunch, or dinner. What with the awful dresses in the store across the street, the yucky-smelling entryway, the moaning sex from the rooftop that was supposed to be reserved for twilight v&t's with Vanessa while they planned a way to sabotage Serena's run for senior speaker, Blair had had *enough*. She dug into her Fendi purse and grabbed her cell phone, pressing the buttons frantically.

"Blair darling? To what do I owe the pleasure, chica?" Chuck Bass answered in a loud voice, sounding more gay than usual. "Don't tell me, you've secretly been in love with me all these years and now that we're about to graduate, you're finally bold enough to tell me."

"Not exactly," Blair snapped. "You're the only one I know with a car."

"A pearl gray convertible Jag isn't just a car, it's a mobile pleasure den." Chuck tooted the horn in the background. "I happen to be in 'the car' as we speak."

"Whatever." Blair threw open the loose-hinged plywood door to the cramped, mothball-smelling coat closet in the living room and yanked out her two matching brown leather, gold-embossed Louis Vuitton duffel bags. The bags were still partially packed, since Vanessa didn't have enough closet space to accommodate Blair's endless wardrobe. All she had to do was fold in the dresses hanging from the closet rail and fill a shopping bag or four or five with the mere thirty-six pairs of shoes she'd brought with her, and she'd be ready to roll. "Can you come get me?"

"Of course, my sweet." Chuck's voice took on a faux paternal tone. "You're not in any sort of trouble, are you?"

Blair grimaced at the sight of a roach motel camped in the back of the closet, a half-dead roach flailing its hind legs on its doorstep. "I'm in *Williamsburg*," she wailed, as if she were being held hostage in somebody's basement.

"And Manhattan *needs* you," Chuck intoned. "*We absolutely need you!*"

Blair giggled. It felt good not pretending anymore that she was going to become one of those hipster girls who wore striped kneesocks and vintage kilts and kooky glasses, ate hummus all the time, and went to art galleries after school instead of to Barneys. She pulled her favorite red-and-white polka-dotted Diane von Furstenberg wrap dress off its hanger and put it on, shedding her black Habitual jean skirt and boring dark gray C&C California T-shirt. Manhattan needed her. Of course it did.

"I'll be there in five, honey. I'm just getting on the bridge now," Chuck assured her, the Jag's engine roaring in the background. "So, where am I taking you, anyway? Back home?"

Blair hadn't thought about this. Or rather, she had, but home wasn't her first choice. Her mother was still mentally unsound after marrying Cyrus Rose that fall and having his baby daughter that spring. Cyrus was loud and sweaty and obnoxious and preferred to wander the house wearing only a loosely tied green silk robe and nothing else. Baby Yale was adorable most of the time, but she had taken over Blair's room, shunting Blair into Aaron's old room, where Blair's cat, Kitty Minky, had developed a peeing problem in reaction to the scent of Aaron's boxer, Mookie. Speaking of—where *was* Mookie? He usually came with Aaron when Aaron stayed over at Vanessa's instead of sleeping in Blair's brother Tyler's room or passing out on the leather sofa in the penthouse library after too many organic beers.

Nudge, nudge.

"Maybe now that I'm into Yale, I won't mind being at ho . . ."

Blair's voice trailed off as inspiration hit and a new, fabulous idea began to form in her head.

After her father had moved out of the penthouse and before he'd left for France to live with his gay French lover—Jacques or Jean-Claude, or whatever the fuck his name was—he'd camped out at the Yale Club for a few months. It was right across the street from Grand Central Station, but, unlike the old train station, the Yale Club had never really been renovated and still had that shabbily elegant Old New York vibe. It was the type of place Blair's former best friend Serena would adore, while Blair would normally have preferred a more sumptuously elegant suite at the Carlyle or one of the city's other landmark hotels. But she'd already stayed in a suite at the Plaza, where she'd been treated like just another well-to-do guest. At the Yale Club she'd be "Harold Waldorf's daughter," which was almost as good as being royalty.

Almost.

"Actually, I'm moving to the Yale Club—at least until I figure out what I'm doing this summer," she announced into the phone, smiling down at her perfectly manicured coral pink fingernails as if this had been her plan all along.

"Is that so?"

Blair looked up from her overstuffed black Barneys shopping bags full of shoes. Vanessa was standing in the open doorway to the apartment, hands on her pale, round hips, wearing a black wifebeater T-shirt and black cotton Hanes underwear. That scraggly boy Blair thought Vanessa had dumped for good was standing behind her, wearing only a pair of gray Fruit of the Looms, while the rest of his worn-too-often-to-ever-come-clean clothes were bundled in his arms. A huge grapey bruise stood out on his throat, just below his Adam's apple.

Ew—a hickey!

"It's the one with the graffiti all over the door. I'll be

downstairs in five minutes," Blair instructed Chuck before hanging up. She put her hands on her hips, trying to think of a nice way to tell Vanessa that she was out of there. It was amusing being friends with the shaven-headed girl everyone in her class thought was so weird, and Blair genuinely liked Vanessa for her no-bullshit approach to everything and her dark, sarcastic sense of humor. But as graduation approached, Vanessa had grown slightly manic—asking Blair to paint her toenails on an almost nightly basis and even getting Blair to try that stupid brush-on hair-highlighting kit with her. Thank God it had only been temporary. Vanessa seemed to crave company, so if two-timing Blair's stepbrother, Aaron, with this straggly Dan guy made her happy, Blair honestly didn't care. She personally was through with men. In just a few short minutes, Vanessa would have the apartment all to herself again—she could go ahead and have a full-fledged orgy if she wanted to.

"Someone's coming to pick me up," she said in lieu of an explanation.

Vanessa had just been caught cheating on Blair's stepbrother, Aaron, with Dan, who was supposed to be history. Most people would have acted at least slightly sheepish in such a situation. Not Vanessa. She blinked her big brown eyes accusingly at Blair. "You're leaving? How come? Are you pissed at me?" She cocked her shaved head and corrected herself. "I mean, more than usual?"

To call Blair and Vanessa the Odd Couple was an understatement. Blair had been raised by a team of nannies and had attended preschool at Park Avenue Presbyterian, just like all the other children from the best Upper East Side families. Vanessa had been raised by her hippie artist parents in Vermont and been homeschooled until the age of ten. She'd moved to Williamsburg to live with her older sister, Ruby, at the age of fifteen and had spent her first two summers working double shifts at the local Kinko's copy shop to earn enough money to buy her first digital video camera. Blair had spent her summers playing tennis on her father's estate in Newport, Rhode Island, or helping Serena filch bottles of Stoli out of the liquor cabinet in Serena's Ridgefield, Connecticut, country house. Blair modeled herself after Audrey Hepburn, and her favorite color was bright pink. Vanessa modeled herself after no one, except maybe the great Swedish avant-garde filmmaker Ingmar Bergman, and wore only black. They couldn't have been more different.

"No." Blair shrugged, allowing a small smile to play on her foxlike face. "Why would I be mad?"

Vanessa padded into the kitchen and retrieved one of the waterlogged tofu pups Aaron had left in the pot on the stove, eating half of it in one bite. She'd developed a taste for them since hooking up with Aaron. "Want one?" she offered both Blair and Dan, waggling it at them like a chewed-on finger.

Gee, thanks.

"I'm good," Dan mumbled, fumbling with his rumpled pants.

Blair flapped her hands at the tofu pup, the half-naked Dan and his icky hickey, the dingy-despite-its-new-coat-of-paint apartment, and all of Williamsburg outside. "It's just not me," she tried to explain.

Vanessa nodded slowly. Ever since Blair had found Serena and Nate colluding in the pool house bathtub at Isabel Coates's Hamptons beach house, she'd been acting a little manic. "Are you sure the Yale Club will even take you? It's not like you're an alumna yet."

Blair shoved an armload of jewel-toned Juicy Couture tracksuits into her already-heaving duffel bag. She used to be so sensitive about the subject of Yale, but that was before she got in. "My dad's a member. They'll take me or he'll kick their asses."

Vanessa was still watching her. Blair could hear the ticking of the electric clock on the old stove. "Oh. I almost forgot."

She picked up the Browns of London shopping bag she'd lugged all the way home from school.

Not that she'd actually walked all the way.

"I got you a dress for graduation. It was too perfect, and I figured you didn't know where to buy anything that isn't black. I even have the perfect shoes you can have to go with it."

Vanessa tugged the white-tissue-wrapped bundle out of the bag and shook out the dress. Even though it was white, it was awesome. Sort of Morticia-Addams-meets-Bride-of-Frankenstein. Of course, she didn't have the heart to tell Blair that Aaron had proposed they leave town before graduation even happened.

And we thought she'd forgotten all about that.

Vanessa stood on one foot and scratched the back of her calf with the black-painted toenails of her other foot, still holding the dress. She was already freaking out about graduating and what lay ahead, and now this. "Shit. This is sad." She threw her arms around Blair. "I'm going to miss you."

Blair hugged her back. "Look, we're practically the same height," she murmured gently, giving Vanessa's doughy half-naked body an affectionate squeeze. "We'll totally be next to each other in the graduation lineup."

Vanessa smiled and wiped away a stray tear. She pointed to one of the myriad pairs of Manolo stilettos scattered on the dusty wooden floor. "Not when you wear those."

"Well, you can always borrow a pair," Blair offered gently. The two girls laughed, and in an instant all was forgiven. Even the loud sex with Aaron last night and the random sex with Dan on the roof in what was supposed to have been Blair and Vanessa's special spot. If that was what she needed to do to fend off pregraduation jitters, then so be it.

"I'm going to take a shower," Dan announced, even though neither of the girls was paying any attention to him.

Vanessa picked up the black jean skirt Blair had discarded

on the floor and pulled it over her butt without even attempting to button it. Then she slung the handles of one of the Louis Vuitton duffel bags and two of the Barneys bags full of shoes over her shoulder. "Come on. I'll help you carry your bags downstairs."

Chuck was waiting on the corner behind the wheel of his new silver convertible Jag—an early graduation present. The car looked completely incongruous with the funkily run-down neighborhood. He popped open the trunk and the girls dropped Blair's bags inside.

"I left some other stuff for you in the closet." Blair gave her classmate a quick hug. "See you tomorrow in English."

Vanessa hugged her back. "See you tomorrow, bitchface," she answered tenderly.

Blair watched the graffitied door slam closed behind her as Vanessa went inside. Then she opened the Jag's passenger-side door.

"I heard that back in the forties all the alums used to keep prostitutes at the Yale Club," Chuck announced as Blair reached for her seat belt. "And they didn't even have a ladies' room." He pulled away from the curb and slipped his hand over Blair's bare knee. "I knew it would never last. You're a boy's girl, not a girl's girl."

Blair shoved his hand away and rolled her blue eyes in annoyance. Chuck was and always would be a slimeball, tolerated only because he and Blair and the rest of their ilk had all been born at Lenox Hill Hospital at Seventy-seventh and Park and had all gone to nursery school together. They'd attended dancing school together and vacationed with their families in St. Barts. Their parents were on the boards of the Metropolitan Museum and the Metropolitan Opera, and they all spoke the same unspoken language. But unlike his other Upper East Side cohorts, Chuck had failed to get into any of the private colleges he'd applied to. His parents were sending him to a random military academy in northern New Jersey instead. So it was easy to understand why he was so critical of the Yale Club: He was a teensy bit jealous.

You think?

Justin Timberlake's new CD was playing on the Blaupunkt car stereo, and Blair turned it up as loud as it would go. Chuck put his hand on her knee again as they approached the Williamsburg Bridge. She picked it up and put it on the gearshift. Had Chuck confused her with a slut like Serena, who had no morals and would fool around with a boy just because he was good-looking and she was vaguely horny? "Drive," she ordered. "Just drive." She folded her hands primly in her lap. She wasn't like that.

Oh, wasn't she?

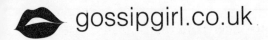
gossipgirl.co.uk

Disclaimer: All the real names of places, people, and events have been altered or abbreviated to protect the innocent. Namely, me.

hey people!

Don't know much about nothing but s-e-x

Finals are next week and no one seems to care. Instead of staying in and memorizing time lines for AP American history or irregular conjugations for French, everyone's staying in, ordering Chinese food, and going to bed . . . with a friend. We're such a predictable bunch. But what better way to get rid of prefinals and pregraduation stress?

Did someone mention gifts?

Graduation—the actual ceremony, I mean—is really for the parents. The gifts we get for graduating make sitting through it totally worthwhile. Let's guess what some of our favorite people are asking Mom and Dad for. . . .

B: She claims to be over men, but what she really wants is a new hunky boyfriend. One that wouldn't cheat on her with her best friend at a party in a bathtub.

V: An alternative-boy calendar so she can keep them all straight.

N: A lifetime supply of Kleenex with a nice blue plaid Ralph Lauren Kleenex-box holder.

D: A used Hyundai, a driver's license . . . oh, and a life.

S: A hobby other than stealing her best friend's boyfriend. Whatever happened to her modeling/acting career, anyway?

J: Wait, she's not graduating. But she still needs a school to go to next year.

Something we all want: a single gigantic, fantabulous party for everyone to go to. None of that irritating never-get-to-finish-your-drink party-hopping business. Let's just find the perfect venue, invite everyone, have the time of our lives, and never leave.

your e-mail

dear GG,
my little brother is in the ninth grade at st. jude's and he heard that **N** is going to a shrink. supposedly he has to, like, regress back to being a baby so his shrink can figure out why he's such a pothead. that's why he's crying all the time.
—nformed

Dear nformed,
Forgive me for asking, but doesn't this regression technique also cause **N** to wet his pants? Ew. Poor guy!
—GG

Sightings

N kissing **S** demurely on the cheek outside her apartment building at Eighty-second and Fifth. Were her parents watching, or is he, like, the only boy in the entire universe who can actually resist her, even though she's supposedly his girlfriend? Maybe he had soggy pants and he had to hurry home and change? **B** and **C** blasting music in traffic on the **Williamsburg Bridge**. His arm was around her and she was petting his monkey. Now *there's* a relationship that could work! **V** spraying her rooftop love den with air freshener and rearranging the fur throw pillows. With so many guys to pick up after, it must be hard to keep things tidy and smelling fresh. And was that a pair of boys' tighty-whiteys we saw her toss off the roof to the street?! **J** in a **New Hampshire** hardware store trying to talk her dad out of buying a wheelbarrow for **D** as a joke graduation present instead of a car. Don't think he'd appreciate the joke. **K** and **I** trying on every pair of white flats **Ferragamo** makes. Is someone going to tell those girls that wearing matching shoes is tacky? Hey look, I just did!

Remember, graduation is really for the moms and dads. So why not wear that frilly **Laura Ashley** dress with the enormous white bow over the butt that your mom has been saving for you since you were ten and then reap the rewards. Can you spell *B-M-W*, anyone?

Excuse my greed.

You know you love me.

gossip girl

s demonstrates how to be naughty and nice

"Mr. Beckham?" Serena called, tugging open the first of four heavy black curtains that led into Constance Billard's darkroom. "Mr. Beckham, is it okay if I come in and talk to you for a minute?"

Serena heard a stool squeak. "Sure thing, come on in," Constance Billard's only film teacher called back. "Careful with the curtains."

Classes were over for the day, and a quiet hung over the school, broken only by the laughter of a few stray girls or the click of a teacher's heels. Serena had stayed behind to see if she could remedy the whole senior-class-speaker situation. Not that she'd definitely get it, but she'd taken enough away from Blair already. Becoming senior class speaker would just be one more thing she got without really wanting it.

Like a certain green-eyed boyfriend?

She slipped inside the darkroom, making sure the curtains swung closed behind her to block out every bit of light. A special red darkroom lamp glowed overhead, but it was still hard to see. Goosebumps appeared on Serena's bare arms and legs. The darkroom always gave her the chills.

Mr. Beckham was the only cool young male teacher at Constance. Except he thought he was cooler, younger, and better looking than he actually was. Fancying himself an artist, he wore chunky black rectangular glasses and tight black long-sleeved Club Monaco T-shirts that showed off his gym-toned chest. He spiked his dark blond hair with gel and inserted the odd French word whenever he could.

"Ah, Serena," he exclaimed, pushing away the poppy-seed bagel with cream cheese he'd been snacking on. He spread his arms out wide. "Quelle pleasure!"

Serena fiddled with the button on the waistband of her light-blue-and-white seersucker spring uniform skirt and shifted from foot to foot. Why was talking to a teacher outside of class always slightly embarrassing?

Especially when you suspected the teacher had a teensy-weensy crush on you.

"Um, I just wanted to thank you for nominating me for senior speaker," Serena told him. She stuck her thumb in her mouth and began gnawing on its already chewed-on pearly pink nail.

Note to all: Only ridiculously beautiful people can get away with this sort of behavior without grossing everyone else out.

"Anyway," she continued, "I just wanted you to know that I crossed myself off the list of nominees." She moved on to her ring finger, which hadn't been chewed on since breakfast. "I've never been that good at making speeches."

Plus, Blair is the only other person nominated, and she really wants to do it, and I'm afraid if I get it she might murder me in my sleep.

Mr. Beckham took off his glasses and began to clean them with the bottom of his black T-shirt, revealing a bare patch of surprisingly buff stomach. Serena tried not to stare and wondered fleetingly if he was gay. His bare skin seemed totally indecent, like he was flashing her or something.

"You know why I nominated you, *n'est-ce pas?*" he asked, looking searchingly at her in the red darkness as he continued to clean his glasses.

Mais oui. Because you have le hots pour elle?

"Well . . ." Serena began, searching for an excuse to turn and flee. There was suddenly something creepy and unsanitary about the fact that Mr. Beckham had been eating a bagel while developing film. She wondered if he was addicted to the chemicals or something.

Mr. Beckham put his glasses back on and sat back on his metal swivel stool. "Serena, I've been watching you since I came here, back when you were only in seventh grade. And I know it sounds corny, but you really lit up my darkroom." He stopped to clear his throat, clearly too nervous to think of any words in French. "If I weren't your teacher, I'd . . ."

He'd . . . pour fixer all over her and lick it off? Some advice: *Run, girl, run!!!!*

Serena was pretty sure she didn't want to hear anything more. "Um, Mr. Beckham? Sorry, but I really have to go. I just wanted to say thanks for being so supportive." She held up her hand and waved stiffly, even though he was sitting right in front of her. "I guess I'll see you at graduation," she added with faux cheerfulness. Then she turned to push her way through the heavy curtains again.

"Wait."

Her stomach filled with dread and she shivered again in her thin white baby tee. She could hear voices outside in the hallway. Someone would hear her if she yelled loudly enough. She turned around. "I really do have to go."

Mr. Beckham slipped off his stool and walked toward her. "May I . . ." He swallowed, his Adam's apple bobbing nervously. "Would you mind if I just . . . gave you a petit, petit kiss?" he asked quietly, pinching together his thumb and forefinger to demonstrate just how small the kiss would be.

Serena hesitated, reluctant to turn this into a huge deal but eager to get rid of him. She could just say no and leave. Or she could freak out and run up to Mrs. M's office and turn him in. Or she could let him give her a little tiny kiss to remember her by and then just forget about it forever.

She shrugged her bony shoulders and turned to offer up her smooth, delicately sun-freckled cheek, making it quite clear that Mr. Beckham wasn't about to get any lip action.

He took a step forward and placed a careful kiss in the middle of her cheek, like a stamp. "*Tant pis,*" he breathed wistfully and then flung open the darkroom curtains, as if to let her know that he had no intention of molesting her any further.

Guess he didn't care much about exposing his film.

"Adieu, Serena."

In the hall just outside the darkroom, Mrs. M stood dressed in her favorite red, white, and blue Talbots linen pantsuit with Ms. D'Agostino, the mousy freshman Spanish teacher, who was holding a gold metal tin full of chocolate truffles. "Ooh, you little she-devil!" Mrs. M cooed delightedly as she popped a truffle into her mouth. Then she noticed Serena and her brown eyes grew wide, like a child caught with her hand in the cookie jar.

Serena fought back a fit of giggles, suddenly feeling like a balloon with too much air in it. How bizarre life was. She grinned at Mrs. M and snatched a truffle from the tin as she hurried toward the school exit.

Oh, the things we seniors get away with. Now, run, baby, *run!!*

The final lacrosse team party of the year was in the St. Jude's gym, which was kind of lame, since it was like eighty degrees outside, and a party in the park would have been much better. But the boys were all underage, and so a few six-packs in the gym and some pizza was all Coach Michaels would allow. Besides, the boys had all gotten high at Jeremy Scott Tompkinson's house beforehand and would all go on to get trashed someplace else afterwards, so what did it matter?

Nate picked at his pizza and squeezed his eyelids shut. The last lax party of the year. The last lax party *ever*. Damn. The tears were already beginning to fall.

The gym was up on the roof of the six-story East End Avenue redbrick school building, with giant plate glass windows overlooking the shimmering East River and Queens. One afternoon near the end of tenth grade, Nate, Jeremy, Anthony Avuldsen, and Charlie Dern had volunteered to put away the gear after lax practice. They'd hung out for a while shooting hoops and then hidden from Rick, the janitor, behind the giant metal rack where the balls were stored. When Rick was done and the lights went out, they'd lined up in front of the windows—right where Nate was standing now—watched the sun set, smoked some weed, and eaten Starbursts until nine. An alarm had gone off when they finally left the building, but they'd sprinted to Carl Schurz Park a few blocks away and had never gotten caught. That had been a good time. Now the good times were about to be over. Maybe they already were.

Nate's eyes scanned the horizon above the silvery water and low industrial buildings. Somewhere southwest of Queens was Williamsburg, Brooklyn, where Blair lived now. He wondered what she was doing. Standing on her roof, maybe, smoking a Merit Ultra Light and sticking thumbtacks into the little voodoo dolls she'd probably made of him and Serena.

Don't flatter yourself, honey.

Nate flicked the tears away from his gorgeous green eyes with his thumb and dropped his barely touched slice of pepperoni pizza into the garbage. Anthony came over, slung his thick-muscled arm around Nate's shoulders, and kissed him on the cheek with mock tenderness. "What's the matter, sweetheart?"

"Fuck off," Nate replied, jabbing Anthony in the ribs.

His friend refused to be shaken off so easily. "Will you just drink a beer with us and stop moping already?" An overgrown hank of white-blond hair swung over Anthony's freckled face and he brushed it away. "Dude, it's party time!"

Nate laughed and allowed himself to be shepherded over to where the other guys were standing, drinking beer and listening to the coach talk. Jeremy hitched up his way-too-big dark blue Levi's and tossed Nate a bottle of Heineken. "Hey, did you hear this? Every Wednesday after practice Coach has been popping Viagra and meeting his wife at the Pierre Hotel." He cracked open another bottle for himself and took a long swig. "Who would have thunk."

Coach Michaels stuck his hands into the pockets of his ever-present red Lands' End windbreaker, looking pleased with himself. "Who says we can't enjoy ourselves?"

Nate raised his bottle in silent answer to the coach's

question and chugged half its contents. Coach Michaels had all the gruff, fatherly qualities a guy could wish for in a coach, but Nate had never had much affection for him. The coach had made him captain halfway into the season only because the junior who was supposed to be captain went mysteriously AWOL from school. And the coach had yet to congratulate Nate on getting into Yale, Brown, *and* Harvard. It didn't surprise Nate that the coach needed Viagra to get it on. He was sort of a cold fish.

Not that Nate was one to judge. After the trunk show at the St. Claire that morning Serena had been all over him, but instead of working up a sweat with her as the cab zoomed up Park Avenue, all he'd been able to do was look out at the grassy divider running down the center of the street, weeping because the heat had caused the red and yellow tulips to scatter their blossoms and wilt.

Guess the tulips weren't the only things wilting.

Coach Michaels started on a tear about how minivans were actually the sexiest cars on the road because they had two sets of backseats. Nate sipped his beer as he reevaluated the coach. Even in his stupid red Lands' End jacket he was healthy, sharp, and vital. No one ever caught *him* crying like a girl at the slightest thing. Maybe a little Viagra was exactly what Nate needed.

Oh, no.

Nate finished off his beer and set the bottle down on the long white collapsible table the school kitchen staff had set up for the party. Then he turned and headed toward the physical education staff office on the other side of the gym, next to the guys' locker room. Everyone would think he was just taking a piss.

When in fact . . .

On Coach's desk was an eight-by-ten photo-portrait of his wife, Patricia. She looked a little like Jennifer Aniston with wrinkles and a dyed-auburn pageboy haircut. Small and leathery, in a magenta-colored Lands' End for Ladies version of Coach's jacket, her brown eyes were shining and her pink, lipstick-free lips were parted in a broad, happy smile. Her teeth were so white they had to be fake, and Nate wondered if she took them out during those Viagra-induced escapades at the Pierre Hotel.

The P.E. department office smelled like stale potato chips and feet. A huge stack of old magazines was on the floor, topped with the swimsuit issue, which sported a picture of some impossibly hot Brazilian chick wearing nothing but what looked like a chain-mail thong. Her freckled arms hugged her bare chest casually, and she was laughing at the camera, as if to say, "Dare me to drop my arms!"

Nate was tempted to pick the magazine up and check it out but he resisted, pulling open the wide drawer beneath Coach's green metal desktop instead. The drawer was a mess, full of those small foil bags of honey-roasted peanuts they pass out on airplanes, bottles of whiteout, bulldog clips, Advil, ice packs, and various vials of prescription medicine. Nate sorted through them until he found the one he was looking for. Casually, he dropped it in his Brooks Brothers khakis pocket and slipped out of the office.

The other boys were still listening to the coach brag about how many times he'd gotten his wife pregnant.

"I was already married by the time I was your age," the coach was saying.

"*Whoa*," Nate's teammates murmured in horror.

Actually, being already married to Blair might have saved him a lot of trouble, Nate thought a little nonsensically.

Right. Like being married would have kept him from cheating on her?

"Yo, Babes!" Jeremy shouted over to Nate. He hitched up his jeans and grabbed another Heineken out of the cooler. "You got a girl hiding in the bathroom or what?"

The other boys looked up expectantly. Despite being a

dumb, handsome jock just like the rest of them, Nate always managed to deliver the most surprises. The mere fact that he'd managed to bag both Blair Waldorf *and* Serena van der Woodsen had raised his status to near-godlike.

Nate smiled weakly and held out his hands, motioning for Jeremy to toss him another beer. If they could have seen what was in his pocket, they would have been very surprised indeed.

a funny thing happened at the yale club

"So good to have you with us, Miss Waldorf," the Yale Club's uptight concierge greeted her. "If you'll just follow me, Dominick will tend to your luggage."

"Thank you," Blair replied graciously, pleased with herself for having made Chuck call and pretend to be her father, booking her a suite only minutes before she arrived. Of course, she could have asked her dad to call himself, but he was in Germany buying a plane or a car—she wasn't sure which—for his new French boyfriend, Giles, and she didn't want to bother him.

The Yale Club lobby was businesslike and unfussy, with a black-and-white marble floor, white walls, and a few Yale-blue wing-back chairs scattered about. Blair kept her chin up as the staff scurried about with her bags and keys, imagining she was Elizabeth Taylor, back in the days when she was beautiful, thin, and glamorous, arriving at some simple bed-and-breakfast in a small town in Scotland where her new film was being shot. She could tolerate the old-fashioned, crusty surroundings so long as she spent most of her time in the bar.

She followed the black-vested, bow-tie-wearing concierge into one of the old wood-paneled elevators and stood silently waiting for the door to close, praying that her suite would have lots of closet space and decent sheets. It was precisely one of those awkward, mundane little moments that made her feel like most of life was just waiting for something to happen.

But then, something *did* happen.

"Hold it!" a tall, broad-shouldered boy shouted as he dashed into the elevator. His light brown hair was short and wavy, and his skin was tanned a nice golden brown color. His glittering green eyes were framed by long, golden brown lashes, and his girlish red mouth was set off by a masculine square chin.

"Cheers," he thanked the concierge in a British accent. Then he turned and stood facing Blair, unabashedly checking her out as the elevator doors rolled shut behind him.

Looks like Elizabeth has found her Richard Burton.

Blair teetered on her gold Manolo Egyptian Goddess sandals as they glided upwards. What a charming British accent. What a beautiful crisp white shirt and perfectly ironed Helmut Lang jeans. What adorable Church's of London tan lace-up shoes. What golden brown hair, what green eyes, what great height! He was like a taller, handsomer version of Nate—but even better than Nate, because of that delicious accent!

Isn't she supposed to be through with men? But a super-British version of Nate? Come on, who could resist?

The elevator stopped on the fourth floor. The boy stood aside, and the concierge stepped out. "If you'll just follow me, miss," he said, motioning to Blair to follow him. Blair hesitated. How could she leave such a delicious-looking boy behind?

"After you, miss," the boy murmured quietly, pressing the door-open button so Blair wouldn't get squashed.

"Right this way," the concierge prompted, leading the way down the Yale blue–carpeted hallway.

Blair stepped out into the hall and began to follow the concierge, walking as slowly as possible. Then suddenly the

boy was walking beside her, exuding pleasant odors and looking delighted with his own hotness.

The concierge stopped at the end of the hallway. "Yours is
the junior suite, miss. Right next to His Lordship's."

His *Lord*ship?!

The English boy smiled at Blair as he fumbled with his
key. "Lord Marcus Beaton-Rhodes," he introduced himself,
thrusting his hand out. Blair noticed right away he was wearing a Yale ring. "Embarrassingly enough, my friends at Yale all
call me Lord."

*Lord. I'd like you to meet my boyfriend, Lord. This is my hus-
band, Lord. We met at Yale. The lord and his gorgeous wife will be
vacationing on their yacht in the South of France this spring with
their perfect family before a long sojourn at their summer castle in
Cornwall. . . .*

"And you are?"

Blair fluttered her thick, mascaraed eyelashes, awakening
from her delicious daydream. "Blair Cornelia Waldorf," she
trilled, sounding exactly like Audrey Hepburn in *Breakfast at
Tiffany's* when she first introduces herself to her new neighbor, Paul Varjak. "Actually, I'm starting at Yale this fall."

"And I've just finished there. Wa-hey!" Lord Marcus
tossed his keys into his room and kicked off his shoes in the
doorway. "Blimey, I'm late for squash, but let's . . ." He
smiled shyly. "Shall we get together for a drink tonight?"

Blair nodded in dumb agreement. She could hardly
believe her luck.

"See you in the lounge at seven, then."

The lord closed his door and the concierge deposited the
adjacent suite's keys into Blair's hand. "Your bags will be here
in a moment. Is everything all right, Miss Waldorf?"

"Bloody hell!" she heard the lord exclaim in his adorable
accent as he crashed around in his suite. Blair imagined him
throwing his beautiful, tailor-made English clothes all over
the place as he hunted for something to wear for squash. If

she were his girlfriend, she'd color-code his shirts for him and alphabetize his shoes according to designer so he wouldn't have to thrash around so much looking for things.

Of course she would.

She stepped inside her room and flopped down on the king-size bed to listen, her eyes darting around the room as she did so, taking it all in. It was small and shabby-chic, erring on the shabby side, the gold accents on the curtains and bedspread and the Regency blue-patterned wallpaper the only attempts at grandeur. It wasn't exactly the Plaza, but there *was* a hot English lord living next door.

Yes, yes—everything was *more* than all right.

what boarding schoolers do when they're bored

It was already five in the afternoon by the time Jenny and her father arrived at the Croton School, in Croton Falls, New York. Rufus's weekly wine and beat poetry night with his weirdo anarchist poet cronies was starting in an hour at a speakeasy in Greenwich Village, and he was getting antsy. Croton was only an hour and a half from the city by train, and Jenny was anxious to ditch him, anyway, so she offered to take the train home.

"Don't get off at 125th Street," Rufus advised, even though the stop was closest to their apartment. He handed Jenny three twenty-dollar bills. "Go all the way to Grand Central and then get a cab. And call me when you're leaving so I can tell your brother when to expect you."

Like Dan really cared if she *ever* came home. Lately Dan had been so preoccupied, he barely seemed to remember that they used to kind of be friends.

Jenny kissed her father on the cheek. It was cute how he babied her, but she was almost fifteen—she could take care of herself. "Have a nice night, Daddy," she told him sweetly. She waved good-bye as the battered navy blue Volvo station wagon disappeared down the road. Then she unbuttoned her blouse another notch and stepped inside a cute red clapboard house with a gold plaque on its hunter-green-painted door that read ADMISSIONS, eager to meet her Croton tour guide.

"You!" a male voice crowed enthusiastically as soon as she opened the door. "It's you!"

Jenny's pretty red mouth dropped open in shock. Leering at her from across the quaintly decorated admissions office reception area was a more masculine, less flamboyantly dressed clone of Chuck Bass. Same European-aftershave-commercial-handsome face, same slicked-back dark hair, same cocky smile, same perverted twinkle in the eye. He walked over and held out his hand, a gold monogrammed pinky ring flashing on his right hand. "I'm your tour guide. Name's Harold Bass. Call me Harry. You may know my cousin Charles Bass—goes by Chuck. He told me all about you. And of course I've seen your pictures on the 'Net."

Oh, God.

Jenny mustered a smile. Chuck Bass had nearly deflowered her in a stall in a ladies' room in the old Barneys building during her first dressy benefit party that fall, and Jenny was still a little scared of him. But the Basses were a powerful Upper East Side family notorious for their philanthropy and decadence and the wild ways of their fucked-up children. If Chuck's cousin liked it at Croton, then it was probably just the sort of school Jenny was looking for.

"Don't be put off by how straitlaced everything seems here, Jennifer," Harry advised, his white teeth flashing. He shoved his hands in the pockets of his cool light blue linen Zegna trousers, which he was wearing with straw flip-flops—very prep-school-boy-goes-to-the-beach. "We basically party, like, eighty percent of the time, sleep fifteen percent of the time, eat five percent of the time, and study whenever we have time left over, which is, like, never."

Jenny grinned. That sounded fine—just fine.

Harry Bass pressed his lips together and cocked his head as if he were sizing her up. "Come on. There are some people I'd like you to meet."

Her heart racing with eager anticipation, Jenny followed him out of the building and down a long sloping pebbled walkway that curved behind a row of pretty brick buildings with black wooden shutters in the windows. The walkway ended in a narrow dirt path that led along the banks of a quaint little duck pond and into the heavily forested woods. "It's just a little bit farther," Harry explained, his flip-flops flapping against his heels.

Jenny hesitated, wondering what on earth the people he wanted her to meet were doing in the middle of the woods. Was she about to be a part of one of those peculiar boarding school traditions she'd read so much about, like bonfires and midnight skinny-dipping? In the middle of the pond a mallard with a dark green head was quacking loudly at a demure brown duck, trying to get her attention. Jenny couldn't help but marvel at how strange it was to have spent a whole day in the country after spending her entire life until now on the island of Manhattan.

"Where are we going?" she called to Harry as she hurried to keep up.

Before he could answer, a girl in a fire-engine red bikini stepped onto the path about fifty feet ahead of them. "Hey, Bass!" She shouted so loudly, the leaves seemed to shake in the trees overhead. "You and your new girlfriend better get your asses over here before we finish all the you-know-what!"

"Coming!" Harry shouted back. He chuckled at Jenny. "Come on. You know you want to."

He even *sounded* like his cousin.

Now that she was sure she and Harry weren't going to be alone in the woods, Jenny felt more confident about following him. It was cooler in the shade of the trees and smelled of wet moss. All of a sudden they came upon a group of five guys and four girls, sitting in a circle, wearing bathing suits or shorts and T-shirts, the rest of their clothes scattered at the base of a nearby tree. Some of them were drinking cans of

Coors, some of them were smoking cigarettes, and all of them looked extremely happy to be there.

The girl in the red bikini—skinny and pale, with long, shiny light brown hair and beautiful hazel eyes—held out her palms to them. "One more minute and you-know-who was gonna come along and nab these," she told them with a bright smile. Jenny stared at the girl's palms, which were dotted with little white pills.

"April, you rock." Harry scooped a tab of Ecstasy out of the girl's hands and popped it in his mouth. "Go on, Jennifer," he urged Jenny, pointing at April's outstretched palms. "The quicker you eat one, the quicker you'll fall in love with me." He grinned devilishly. "I mean, our school."

Oh, really?

Jenny had been offered drugs before. She'd even been stoned once, with Nate Archibald, the first day they'd met, in Sheep Meadow in Central Park. She'd fallen in love with him that day and had stayed in love with him until he broke her heart on New Year's Eve. Probably if she hadn't been stoned, she'd have understood that she and Nate had only just met and that she needed to get to know him a lot better before she kissed him.

She reached out to pinch one of the tabs of Ecstasy out of April's hand with no intention of actually ingesting it. It was so tiny, no one would even notice.

"Yum," she cooed, pretending to be delighted as she cupped her hand over her mouth and let the teeny pill fall past her chin and cascade down into her ample double-D-sized cleavage.

We always knew it would come in handy!

"We were about to play Duck, Duck, Goose," one of the Coors-drinking guys announced with a completely straight face, as if he were trying to organize a friendly touch-football scrimmage. He was wearing nothing but a pair of electric blue bike shorts, and he looked like a Tour de France bicycle racer, with ropy muscles, a shaved head, and intense blue eyes. "Wanna play?"

"Sure!" Harry Bass responded enthusiastically. He wrapped his arm around Jenny's waist and kissed the top of her head. "My little cucumber," he murmured affectionately.

Jenny had the feeling the tab of E Harry had just taken was not his first of the afternoon. She was about to shrug him away when she realized that she was going to have to at least *pretend* she was on Ecstasy; otherwise, it would be obvious she hadn't taken it. Problem was, she didn't even know how long it was supposed to take to start working. "Yay!" she squeaked. "Let's play!"

They joined the circle and sat down between a chubby Japanese boy sporting Madras plaid Bermuda shorts and a cute rocker haircut and the muscular boy in the blue bike shorts. Everyone was grinning so hard, it looked like their teeth hurt. "I'll go first," April volunteered. "But first I think we're going to need some of this." She passed around a few packets of cinnamon Dentyne gum.

"You're a goddess," blue bike shorts boy told her appreciatively. He shoved three pieces of gum into his mouth and began to chew them voraciously. "Mwa, mwa, mwa!"

April cracked tiny pink bubbles with her gum and then clapped her hands together. "Okay, people, let's go!" She wound her way around to the outside of the circle and began to walk counterclockwise, tapping each person on the head as she passed. "Duck, duck, duck, duck, duck, duck, *goose!*" she shouted as she tapped the Japanese guy with the cool haircut on the head and then sprinted away. He jumped to his feet and gave chase, catching her in his arms and wrestling her to the ground. They lay like that for a while, panting and sort of petting each other.

Jenny noticed that none of the other kids were even watching them. They were too focused on their gum-chewing, or they were rubbing their hands up and down each other's backs and giggling. Then she felt a hand on her back, too, underneath her shirt.

"Let's take our shirts off," Harry suggested eagerly.

"Okay," Jenny agreed, not wanting to be a prude. She only had three buttons left buttoned, anyway. The guidebooks were definitely right about Croton. It was wild, and maybe—once she got used to it—exactly what she needed.

"Wow," he murmured as she folded her shirt neatly and placed it on the grass beside her. The look on his face was the absolute definition of the phrase *to gawk*.

"Now you," Jenny said, feeling confident in the knowledge that she was the only sober one in the forest. Well, *almost*.

"What the hell are you kids doing back here?!" a deep voice boomed. An athletic-looking man with curly brown hair and a brown mustache strode down the path, barefoot, wearing faded Levi's and a threadbare light blue oxford shirt, unbuttoned to midchest.

April sat up and wiped her mouth, her brown eyes shining. "Hi, Mr. Tortia."

Mr. Tortia didn't look as angry as he'd sounded. He almost looked like he wanted to hang out. "So, what did I miss?" he demanded eagerly. Then he noticed Jenny. "And who, may I ask, are you?"

Harry rubbed the spot between Jenny's bare shoulder blades. "She's a prospective. And I think maybe she took your share."

Jenny crossed her hands over her chest. Actually, his share of the E was somewhere inside her nude-colored Bali extra-support bra with double-duty underwire and chafe-free superwide straps, but she wasn't about to volunteer that information.

Mr. Tortia picked something out of his tobacco-stained teeth and flicked it angrily into the grass, looking genuinely pissed off. "This is a school, not a strip club. Put your clothes back on," he snapped at Jenny.

Gladly.

Jenny snatched up her pretty Japanese-style shirt, rising to her feet as she slipped her arms inside the sleeves and buttoned it up to her chin. *Who the hell is this guy, anyway?* she wondered with frightened indignation.

"You can't be serious about attending this institution," Mr. Tortia observed, his thick brown mustache slick with sweat and spittle. "Croton prides itself on its discretion. Our students are the crème de la crème!"

Jenny gazed down at the circle of Croton students, their bare navels and nipples blinking up at her in the warm summer sun, their mouths working the Dentyne, blissed out from the Ecstasy, and exhausted by a single round of Duck, Duck, Goose. Discretion? Crème de la crème? The crème de la crème of fuckups, maybe. And what right did this dude with the mustache have to tell her whether she could go there or not?

"Are you a teacher here or. . . ?" she asked politely.

Mr. Tortia squatted down and held his palm out to April, who handed him a piece of Dentyne. He stood up again. "As a matter of fact, I'm the headmaster," he replied flatly. He pulled on his mustache and offered her his first smile. "Discretion lesson number one: Let's not mention this little incident to anyone. Got it?"

Jenny nodded mutely.

Mr. Tortia held up both hands and waved with his palms facing backwards, like the Queen of England. "Arrivederci, little prospective girl!" he chimed, dismissing her.

Harry reached up and patted Jenny on the bottom. "Drive safely," he told her affectionately, even though she was obviously not old enough to drive.

Arrivederci, fuckups!

Her whole body trembling with outrage, Jenny hurried down the path through the woods, wishing with all her heart there was a subway stop right there by the duck pond. She could swipe her MetroCard and catch the 3 train down to Ninety-sixth Street and Broadway, and be home in time for *American Idol*. The green-headed mallard quacked at her mockingly as she hurried by. "Crème de la crème! Crème de la crème! Crème de la crème!" he seemed to be saying.

Jenny whipped out her cell phone and dialed information. "Taxi. In Croton Falls, New York," she instructed.

"We have no listings for Taxi," the operator responded blandly. "I'll check Limousines."

"Fine." Jenny typed the number for the Village of Croton's only limousine service into her cell phone. With the money her father had given her combined with the money already in her wallet, she could probably get the driver to take her all the way home.

Who said she wasn't the crème de la crème?

v experiments with double happiness

When Aaron came home from band practice Vanessa was standing in front of the bathroom sink, contemplating her hair—or lack thereof—in the round, toothpaste-spattered mirror, still wet from her shower. She'd ridded herself of Dan's musty smell and was horrified to discover that she sort of enjoyed the fact that Aaron had absolutely no clue.

When she's bad, she's *bad*.

"Nice towel," Aaron observed, planting a kiss on the nape of her neck.

"Thanks." Vanessa batted her eyes and placed her hands on her hips, modeling the lavender-and-black chintz floral bath towel, one of the many Blair had purchased for the apartment during her short but sweet stay.

Aaron wrapped his arms around Vanessa's waist. "Did you get my present?"

He looked cute in an orange T-shirt and baggy green army shorts, and he smelled like hay from the herbal cigarettes he was always smoking.

"Blair moved out," Vanessa told him evenly, ignoring his question about the cheesy love/friendship ring he'd left on the kitchen counter that morning. "She couldn't stand living so far away from Barneys in a walk-up with graffiti on the door."

"Well, can you blame her?" Aaron smiled at their reflection

in the mirror—two dark shaved heads, two pairs of brown eyes, two pairs of thin red lips. "Did you get my e-mail?"

We could almost be twins, Vanessa thought, creeping herself out. She was suddenly reminded of those freaky old V.C. Andrews books she'd read when she was twelve, about a brother and sister who were locked together in an attic and eventually gave birth to twins. "Blair wants to be our senior speaker. If I miss graduation, she'll kill me."

Aaron rolled his eyes, flipped the cracked white toilet seat lid down, and sat down on it. He sighed. "I don't know how she does it."

"What do you mean?" Vanessa couldn't help observing that this little bathroom chat was the longest they'd ever talked without forgetting what they were talking about and ripping each other's clothes off.

"You're like the most righteous person I know, but she even manages to get you to do her bidding." Aaron explained, rubbing the back of his neck where the supershort shaved bits were growing in.

"It's not like that. We're friends. Anyway," Vanessa quickly changed the subject. "I think driving across the country and camping out and stuff sounds . . . cool." She put her hands in her pockets, hoping that Aaron would forget all about the ring. "I mean, as long as there's, like, a bathroom and a shower we can use."

Sounds like she doesn't quite know the meaning of "camping out."

"Really?" Aaron stood up, grinning as he turned her around to face him. "So, are you, like, completely naked underneath that towel?" he asked, kissing her neck and shoulders.

Vanessa knew she ought to have been overwhelmed by her outrageous deception. Dan had left only an hour ago. Now here she was with Aaron, her real boyfriend, pretending it was perfectly natural to be taking a shower in the late afternoon, when she normally only took one in the morning. Maybe she was just losing her mind, but somehow it made being with Aaron *and Dan* all the more exciting.

Aaron turned on the shower and pulled his shirt off over his head. "I say we both need to get really, really clean." He tugged on Vanessa's towel. "Come on, I'll wash your hair for you."

The towel fell to the floor and Vanessa laughed out loud, amazed at how unguilty she felt. The truth was, in the very near future she wouldn't be seeing much of these boys at all, so why not enjoy them now, while they were standing right in front of her—naked?

After their steaming hot shower, Aaron busied himself cooking wheat gluten chicken nuggets with sweet potato fries, while Vanessa edited her final film project, a series of interviews with seniors from Constance and other private schools that she'd filmed over the course of the past few months.

Some of the interviews were funny and insightful, but some of them could be interpreted in kind of a bad way if you didn't know the people. She decided to start with Blair's interview. Blair looked totally awesome sitting in front of Bethesda Fountain in Central Park wearing a black polo shirt and her jade-and-Swarovski-crystal chandelier earrings. A group of shirtless boys were playing Frisbee in the background, girls in bikinis sprawled at their feet.

"For me it's not just about having sex, though. It's about my whole future. Yale and Nate: the two things I've always wanted . . ." Blair declared, sounding unusually psychotic. "And if I don't get in . . . someone is going to fucking pay. This is, like, my one chance to be happy, and I think I deserve it, you know?"

Well, hello, crazy bitch.

Vanessa winced. Of course it was good film, but considering how things had turned out with Nate, it would hurt Blair's feelings too much to use it.

Aaron came out of the kitchen to peer over her shoulder at the little screen on her digital video camera, a carrot stick in his mouth. "When's my part?"

Vanessa fast-forwarded until she got to Aaron's interview, taken late one night in her bedroom—which explained why he was wearing only a lavender-and-celery-green striped sheet. The interview had been done before he cut his hair, and brown mini dreadlocks stuck out in all directions from his head.

"I've been feeling really, really good about myself since I heard from Harvard," the practically naked, dreadlocked Aaron told the camera. "I mean, I used to be this skinny kid with braces and frizzy hair, and now I'm, like, the *king*. It totally rocks!"

Good for you, dude. Good for you.

Behind them, the timer on the oven went off. "I sound like an asshole," Aaron observed casually as he headed back into the kitchen. "But you can use it. I don't mind."

Vanessa went back to Blair's segment, watching it over and over and trying to edit it in such a way that Blair wouldn't sound totally demonic. Maybe Blair didn't have Nate anymore, but she had gotten into Yale in the end. As she scrolled over and over through the footage in her film, listening to her classmates' and peers' hilariously self-absorbed statements and sad truths, she grew more and more reticent about missing graduation. Not that she was actually into group hugs or white dresses, but it seemed kind of *wrong* to miss out on the one day she'd been waiting for since she started at Constance Billard in ninth grade.

Like hooking up with two guys on the same day *wasn't* wrong?

Professor Pierre Papadametriou
English Dept., The Evergreen State College
2700 Evergreen Parkway NW
Olympia, WA 98505

Daniel Humphrey
815 West End Avenue, Apt. 8D
New York, NY 10024

Dear Daniel Humphrey,
I was so excited with hiring you for my summer assistant, I forgot to tell you the subject of my book: sex poems. I mean, poems that are about making sex through the ages, which is interesting to me because I teach poetry and biology, and I am Greek! The book has no title yet but maybe you will help me think of a good one! I also did not explain that you will live in my small home with my two dogs, Plato and Plato Jr., and my son, Mick, because Evergreen does not allow students to move in until orientation in end of August. Hammock in attic is fixed, so come! We will make a good time with Micky's homemade ouzo!

Sincerely,
Pierre

d chooses real sex over sex poems

Dan sat in the back of AP English class, his hands trembling as he reread the letter. Professor Papadametriou sounded like a nice man, and he'd probably make a good advisor. Dan could totally picture enjoying a few glasses of wine in the professor's home while he talked about the fall of Troy and his son stuffed grape leaves or whatever. The thing was, Dan didn't want to go to Evergreen at all anymore.

"Dan, could you enlighten us as to who the narrator is in this poem?" Ms. Solomon asked. She was wearing a tight black lace mini tank dress, her nearly translucent, thin, spidery arms and bony legs poking out of it, making her look like a cartoon witch in a Halloween TV special. She wound a strand of mousy dark blond hair around her index finger, a gesture she probably thought was irresistible to Dan. Ms. Solomon had a serious crush on him, and whenever she suspected he wasn't paying attention in class, she stomped her feet like a petulant child and asked him a question, demanding his attention.

He wasn't even sure which poem she was talking about, although he knew it was Robert Frost, and he'd memorized most of Frost.

"It's either the guy or the horse," Dan answered mechanically without even looking up.

"Thanks, Stormfield," Ms. Solomon cracked sarcastically.

"Even I could do better than that," Chuck Bass jeered from the front of the room, where he'd decided to sit every day up until the final exam, in his last-ditch effort to get better than a D in English. Chuck was wearing orange-and-white plaid Bermuda shorts, a white polo shirt, white patent leather shoes, and a matching white patent leather belt. It was the sort of outfit a Park Avenue mom would dress her three-year-old son in for church, only Chuck had chosen the outfit himself. Sweetie sat in Chuck's lap, wearing a tiny rhinestone tiara.

Dan shrugged. He was beyond Chuck's nasty wisecracks, and beyond Ms. Solomon's insolent crush. Way beyond. In fact, right now he was so consumed with love for Vanessa, he wasn't sure what to do with himself.

Uh-oh.

On the subway he'd started writing his graduation speech, modeling it after all the stupid graduation speeches he'd heard in movies. *We are the future. The ticket to a successful life is a good education. The world awaits us with all it has to teach.* But that had been before he and Vanessa had sex on her roof. Now he was pretty sure he was changing the topic. For how could he not write about *love*?

Double uh-oh.

He glanced down at the letter again, picked up his chewed-on black Paper Mate pen, and turned to a clean sheet of paper in his loose-leaf binder.

Dear Professor Papadametriou,

Thank you for offering me the opportunity to work with you this summer. However, something has come up and I will not be able to accept the position. I would very much like to meet you and your dogs and your son sometime. Until then, good luck, and good luck with your book.

All the best,
Daniel Humphrey

P.S. I've enclosed a poem you might want to include in your book.

He turned to another fresh page.

view from the roof

The view is better from up here.
See her factories, her rivers.
If her hills weren't in the way
I could see into the windows of the apartment across the street.
See a woman pouring milk as she sets the table for dinner.
Oh there. There's the table. There.
I can see everything from here.
There. Yes. Right there.

Dan wasn't sure if he really had the guts to send such a sexually explicit poem to a professor he'd never even met, but it would be cool if Professor Papadametriou actually used the poem in his book.

Ms. Solomon sat down at her desk and rested her pointy, unpleasant chin in her hands, looking completely defeated because she'd worn her sexiest dress just for Dan and he'd barely looked at her for the last forty minutes.

"I'd like you to open your notebooks and take the last ten minutes of class to write whatever you feel like writing," she instructed with unusual generosity. Normally she droned on about Wordsworth or some other dead poet until five minutes after the bell had rung, driving the boys apeshit. Dan took the opportunity to get started on a new graduation speech.

Ladies and gentlemen, we are gathered here today to celebrate the end of the first chapter in our lives and the beginning of the second. We already know what comes next. Four years of college, and then another graduation. But whoop-dee-doo! Now is the time to be in love. . . .

Whoop-dee-doo? Triple, super-duper uh-oh.

who's that boy?

Senior homeroom was last period on Tuesday in the Constance Billard senior lounge, a windowless room above the library that had been a storage area until it was given to the seniors as a place to relax and escape from all the underclassmen. No teacher was present, which meant that none of the girls were paying any attention to Mimi Halperin, the perky but lame president of the senior class, as she made announcements about senior privileges during exam week.

"No uniforms all week, girls. And we only have to come to school for our exams. Awesome, huh?" Mimi clapped her chubby hands together and pushed her thick black hair behind her weirdly small ears. The other girls yawned and looked at their watches, eager to leave so they could continue their quest for the perfect graduation dress or work on their tans. Mimi had been the class clown and everyone's buddy way back in third grade, but now that they were all grown up, no one thought she was funny. Still, they'd voted for her for president at the end of junior year because she was the only one who seemed to want to do it. Because it went on your transcript for college, class president was a coveted position, up until senior year. The class president had to attend weekly student council meetings at 7:30 A.M. and help out at all the school functions, like the book fair and the scholarship fund drive. It was a lot of work, and now that it was the end of senior year and everyone was already into college, no one cared.

"Moving on, I'm pleased to announce—drumroll, please—our senior class graduation speaker is . . . Blair Waldorf! Yay, Blair!!" Mimi jumped up and down on her stubby legs and clapped her hands over her head like this was the best thing that had ever happened.

Take that, you bitch! Blair gloated silently at the back of Serena's pale blond head. *That's what you get for trying to sabotage me.*

The lounge hummed with gossip as everyone discussed the results. No one had really wanted Blair to be speaker, because her whole speech was going to be about herself, but they questioned Serena's ability to write a coherent speech.

"She's so dumb from all the drugs she did up at boarding school, she'd probably have to bribe Blair to write the speech for her anyway," Laura Salmon whispered to Rain Hoffstetter.

"I heard Serena dropped out," Rain whispered back. "Nate gave her some gross STD and she's going to miss graduation anyway because she has to go to some clinic in Belgium to try and get cured."

"Is that true?" Blair wondered out loud. Not about the STD part, but about the dropping-out-of-the-running-for-senior-speaker part. She was reluctant to prolong homeroom, because there were only five more minutes left for her to get changed, powdered, glossed, and perfumed before she was scheduled to meet up with a very hot English lord who'd promised to spend the afternoon dress shopping with her. Last night over Ketel One martinis, Lord Marcus had confessed that his squash game had been a total disaster because he'd been thinking about her the whole time. And Blair had confessed to Googling him the minute she'd unpacked her laptop. His family, the Beaton-Rhodeses, owned the largest textile mill in England and lived in a very huge and historical old mansion outside of London. They also owned a villa near Milan and a beach compound in Barbados. Marcus's parents were special friends of the royal family, and Marcus himself had even attended Princess Diana's funeral. He was listed by *Hello!* magazine as one of the most eligible young bachelors in England, and Blair was determined to win his heart before any of those greedy English bitches got to him. But first she needed to know if she'd beaten Serena by getting elected senior speaker or if she'd only won because she was the only girl left in the running. She glared at Serena and repeated, "Is that true?"

Serena squirmed in her seat, pulling her school uniform down over her bare knees and pulling up her pale yellow ankle socks so they looked nerdy and ridiculous. She'd wanted her act of martyrdom to go unnoticed by the rest of the senior class. Now everyone knew about it. "Is there a problem?" she responded, sounding a lot bitchier than she'd intended.

"But Blair, you *want* to be our speaker, right?" Vanessa Abrams asked from her seat right next to Blair's. Vanessa was wearing a black tank top and no bra and should have been sent home for being inappropriate and out of uniform. Normally this sort of go-class-go type of homeroom drove her nuts, but she'd been feeling so nostalgic about graduating lately, she was actually sort of into it.

"Yes," Blair admitted. "I do."

Vanessa rolled her eyes and gave her friend's arm a gentle little shove. "Then what do you care?"

Blair shrugged. "Can we go now?" she asked Mimi, eager to get out of her uniform and into the tight white Juicy Couture clamdiggers and green Marni halter top she'd brought to wear shopping with Lord Marcus.

Serena shot Vanessa a grateful glance. She really hadn't meant to make a fuss. And maybe, when she thought about it later—like, years later, when they both had blue old-lady hair and had retired to Mustique or some other hot and sunny place, Blair might hate her a little less.

After homeroom, the senior girls congregated outside Constance Billard's great blue doors, still buzzing about the senior speaker situation. They couldn't help but notice the gorgeous, tall, golden-haired boy who was standing on the sidewalk only a few feet away, wearing perfectly ironed jeans and the cutest salmon-pink-and-white checked Thomas Pink button-down shirt. Blair brushed by them wearing a completely different outfit from what she'd worn to school that day, sprinted down the steps, and, to their complete amazement, kissed the boy on the cheek without even stopping for air.

"Nice to see you too," Lord Marcus chuckled, holding her arms and looking her up and down appreciatively.

Blair blushed hot pink down to her jade green Kate Spade flats. God, he was dreamy—even better than the boy she'd dreamed up to star opposite her in the movie in her mind, because he was *real*, and *royal*, and more perfect than Nate could ever attempt to be.

Last night at the Yale Club bar, when she'd begun to slur her words from drinking too much Ketel One, he'd held her hand all the way back to their rooms, kissing it gently before he said good night. Blair had swooned so hard she almost puked. How could something so insanely sexy come so effortlessly to him? It had been all she could do to keep herself from sledgehammering the wall between them with her black salon-size Vidal Sassoon hair dryer and jumping his adorable bones.

The group of senior girls clustered in front of the school in their matching light blue seersucker uniforms, looking a little like the pigeons roosting in the eaves of the school roof as they stared incredulously at Blair and her hot British lord.

"What, did she, like, create him in a lab or something?" Laura Salmon demanded with a mixture of jealousy and awe.

She pulled her white eyelet blouse down tight across her chest in a lame attempt to show off her new red DKNY demicup bra.

"He's completely perfect," Isabel Coates breathed, yanking out some of the bobby pins holding down her grown-out brown bangs. "But I bet he, like, washes dishes at the Yale Club or something."

"Actually, I think he's her cousin—you know how she has that aunt in Scotland?" Rain improvised. "She's just pretending he's her hunky new boyfriend to make Nate jealous."

"But Nate's not even here," Kati Farkas pouted, her shiny pink lower lip jutting out in a way that made her look even dumber than she actually was.

"No, but Serena is," Isabel remarked insightfully.

The girls turned to stare at Serena, who had just stepped outside the blue doors. She adjusted the earphones on her pink iPod mini and blinked her gigantic lake-blue eyes, her long, pale blond hair gleaming in the bright, hot sun. She waved to the other girls and then started on her merry way, traipsing down the steps until she caught sight of Blair, hanging on the lapels of her royal British hunk.

Lord Marcus was about to hail them a cab down to the Oscar de la Renta boutique on Madison and Sixty-sixth Street, where he'd promised to help Blair sort out her graduation dress issues, when Blair suddenly grabbed his pink-and-white checked shirt, nearly ripping it off his body.

"Kiss me *now*," she told him urgently. Of course it was sort of unexpected—they'd only just met yesterday—but didn't that make it all the more romantic?

Or all the more bizarre.

"Because somebody's looking or because you want me to?" Lord Marcus responded with an amused, irresistible smile that made it very clear he didn't care either way.

"Both." Blair closed her eyes in anticipation of the kiss. Of course she wasn't in love, *yet*. It was the *idea* of Lord Marcus she loved. But their first kiss lasted longer than an on-screen kiss, tasted better than steak frites, and felt better than a day-dream—*way* better. It certainly wouldn't take much for her to fall genuinely in love. She was definitely almost there.

A cab pulled to a stop beside them and, his lips still pressed against Blair's, Lord Marcus raised his hand to flag it. But the cab was already occupied by a very tense Nate Archibald. Nate opened the cab door, and Lord Marcus and Blair stepped aside to allow Serena to breeze past them and into the backseat. She pulled the door closed, looking up at Blair and Lord Marcus through the window with her huge blue eyes. Blair stared back, her body pressed against Lord Marcus. Serena lifted her hand to wave at them, her perfect lips parting in a smile as the cab took off toward Fifth Avenue.

And even though Serena was already gone, Blair smiled back. Because for once in her life, she honestly didn't give a damn where they were going.

guess who's bonking in bergdorf's?

Located at Fifth Avenue and Fifty-eighth Street, Bergdorf Goodman was one of the oldest and most beautiful luxury department stores in Manhattan. It was the first store Serena's mother had ever taken her shopping in, and even though it was stuffier and more old-fashioned than Barneys or Bendel's, it seemed like the appropriate place to buy her graduation dress. She'd asked Nate to come along only because she needed a second opinion, although with his standard uniform of well-worn knit polo shirts or white button-downs and khakis, Nate wasn't exactly astute when it came to fashion.

"I wonder where Blair met him," Serena mused aloud as Bergdorf's sleek ivory-colored elevator whisked them up to the third floor.

Nate didn't respond. He was staring at Serena's boobs. They were hard looking, like the small Empire apples that grew on his family's estate on Mt. Desert Island, Maine. He had taken a couple of Coach Michaels's Viagras on his way to pick her up and he was pretty sure he was beginning to feel the effect. There was a lot of pressure down there, like a handless hand job, and if he didn't do something about it soon, things were going to get kind of messy.

Like, how soon?

The elevator doors glided open and Serena was immediately

drawn to a rack of exquisitely made white Oscar de la Renta suits—swishy pleated knee-length skirts and fitted jackets with cool white leather belts decorated with adorable little white leather bows.

"I don't know why I even care," she continued as she fingered the suits without even noticing that Nate was staring at her like she was a slice of extra-cheese pizza hot out of a Ray's Original Pizza oven. "Blair will probably never talk to me again."

"May I help you?" offered a bulky middle-aged saleswoman with a gold Bergdorf's name tag that read JOAN. Joan was wearing a purple Chanel suit that did nothing for her lumpy hips and piano legs.

"I need to try these on in a size four." Serena pointed to three of the white Oscar de la Renta suits. Until now she hadn't thought of wearing a suit to graduation instead of a dress, but it seemed to make perfect sense. She'd never been the frilly-white-dress type anyway, and there was something so crisp and final about the suits that made them totally perfect for graduation.

Nate was practically bursting as he followed Serena and Joan to the ladies' fitting room. He stood just outside as Joan hung up the suits, closed the heavy gray velvet curtain, and then hurried off to find something else she thought Serena might like. Now was his chance.

He yanked the curtain open. Serena had unbuttoned her uniform. Her white polo shirt was around her neck and she was wearing only a flimsy white camisole instead of a bra underneath. "Hey," she greeted him with a shy smile. "It's okay if you come in."

Nate yanked the curtain shut with one hand as he unbuckled his belt with the other. *Go, go, go!*

Serena began to remove one of the suits from the hanger. Then she noticed Nate staring at her with his pants around his ankles.

Hello?

"Nate, what are you doing?" His brilliant green eyes glittered and his thin lips parted hungrily, like he hadn't eaten lunch or something. She giggled and crossed her arms over her chest. "They don't have cameras in these things, do they?"

As if either of them cared?

He grabbed her camisole and yanked it away from her body, ripping it entirely in half in the process. Serena dropped the suit on the dressing room floor and grabbed him back. For once, Nate wasn't weeping into a fistful of soggy tissues. She wasn't about to miss this opportunity.

Nate was eternally grateful that Serena was Serena and not Blair. Blair would have wanted to dissect his behavior. She would have wanted to make a fuss or have an argument, while Serena just flicked away the remains of her camisole and helped him off with his shirt. "You didn't tell me you were all hot and bothered."

Slightly.

Nate grabbed the other pristine white satin Oscar suits off their hooks and scattered them at their feet. "Remember when we were in the tub at my house, the summer before tenth grade?" he told her urgently, pressing his lips against her neck.

Serena blushed again. How could she forget? It had been their third time. When they were both still counting.

"Let's do the same thing again," Nate practically shouted. "Pretend all these white dresses are the bubbles!"

Whoa. Who ever said boys lack imagination?

"Yes!"

"Oh, yes!"

"Found something you like, dear?" Joan, ever the helpful Bergdorf sales matron, poked her gray head through the opening in the thick velvet curtain. She stared at the confusion of tanned, writhing limbs and white satin on the floor of the dressing room and then quickly withdrew, popping a few blood pressure pills before attending to a new shipment of Missoni sweaters. That sort of vulgar behavior was completely unladylike and therefore completely un-Bergdorf's, but there wasn't much she could do. Serena van der Woodsen had opened a Bergdorf's charge account when she was seven and had been a loyal customer ever since. And of course it was nice to see that she was so comfortable in the store.

Nate began to cry as soon as it was over. The Viagra had worn off just in time. "I just can't believe you're going to be wearing one of these," he murmured, extracting the skirt to one of the suits from underneath his bare ass.

"Well, I haven't even tried it on yet." Serena let her head fall back, closing her enormous dark blue eyes as Nate pressed his soggy cheek into her hair. It was sweet and sort of feminine of him to cry after they'd done it, and she suddenly realized she was the stronger, more "masculine" one in their relationship. At least they'd finally done it. Now they were more authentically a couple.

That's some couple.

"I already have this yellow Tocca dress I really like, anyway. Maybe I could bleach it or something," she continued distractedly.

Then Nate's mind began to wander, too, to his final history term paper.

Talk about multitasking!

He was writing about the origins of lacrosse, but would his history teacher, Mr. Knoeder, aka Mr. No Dick, think it was un-PC or whatever to write about an old Native American sport without really dealing with the politics of how the Indians had been treated in colonial times and all that? After all, Nate was going to Yale next year to *play* lacrosse, not to become some kind of lacrosse *historian*.

Obviously.

He propped himself up on one elbow and tugged a tissue

out of his navy blue canvas Jack Spade book bag. He'd grown accustomed to carrying tissues.

"Maybe we should have gone to Bendel's to look for dresses instead of here," Serena mused, fingering the buttons on one of the suits.

Nah, their dressing rooms aren't nearly as big.

see *b* die and go to heaven

Why Blair had never been inside the Madison Avenue Oscar de la Renta boutique before was beyond her. The boutique was modeled after Mr. de la Renta's home in the Dominican Republic, with imported Dominican coral stone walls, plaster palm trees, and a shoe display set up like a catwalk. The eveningwear was hung in a special lounge furnished with love seats from de la Renta's furniture collection. Too bad Blair wasn't in the market for a black tulle ball gown or she would have tackled Marcus and pulled him down on one of the toile love seats just to thank him for taking her there.

"Hello, Marthe," Marcus greeted the amazingly beautiful, Amazon-like, Latina saleswoman. She was wearing a gold pouf skirt and a tight, hot pink short-sleeved sweater that were simultaneously fifties retro and ultramodern.

At first Blair's hackles rose and she started to bare her fangs, but then she quickly realized that being jealous of anyone that impossibly tall, curvy, and gorgeous would be a total waste of time.

"Miss Waldorf is looking for a gown in white," Marcus explained, putting his arm around Blair and totally erasing any jealous or irrational thoughts she'd ever had, or ever would have.

Wow, he *is* good.

Marthe nodded seriously and led them to a rack of white goddess gowns that would have looked stunning on Marthe, but that Blair already knew would make her look like a fat runt with no real cleavage to speak of. She was about to protest, but Marcus—bless him—had already figured it out.

"What about one of those suits?" he asked, walking over to finger an exquisite pleated white satin skirt. The skirt was paired with a fitted white satin jacket that sported the most perfect white leather belt around the waist, fastened with a nifty white leather bow.

"You have the perfect figure for his suits," Marthe declared in a wonderful, thick accent. She strode over to the rack and selected three of the suits for Blair to try on. "And you are a size four, I am sure."

"Maybe she is even a size two," a sonorous male voice chimed in from behind them.

Blair whirled around, her heart already aflutter at being mistaken for a size two, and nearly choked on her own saliva when she saw who it was. Standing just a few feet away from her was Oscar de la Renta himself, wearing a perfectly tailored gray suit, a starched white shirt, and a pink tie, his handsome bald head looking like it had been oiled with olive oil, his gray-black eyebrows smoldering. Blair had seen him hundreds of times in the pages of fashion magazines and in the society columns but never in person. And for an old man, he was supremely sexy.

"Ah, Mr. de la Renta," Marthe greeted her boss with a warm smile. "Miss Waldorf will wear your suits well, no?"

Mr. de la Renta looked Blair up and down and then flashed her an appreciative smile. "Very well," he agreed. He turned to Marcus. "I missed your mother in Milan."

"Hello, Uncle Oscar." Marcus smiled broadly, stepped forward, and embraced the designer, hugging him affectionately. Blair nearly threw up all over the beautiful floor.

Uncle Oscar!?

Marcus chuckled and then touched her arm. "He's not really my uncle, but he may as well be. My mother won't wear anything but the clothes Uncle Oscar makes for her."

Who could blame her?

For once, Blair was speechless. She felt exactly like Dorothy in *The Wizard of Oz* when she wakes up after the Kansas cyclone and finds herself in Munchkinland, confronted by Glinda, the beautiful, good witch. Except that Blair wasn't nearly as fat as Judy Garland. *She* was a size *two*!

"This way, Miss Waldorf," Marthe instructed, leading the way to a large jade green–curtained dressing room. She hung up four suits on the hooks inside—two in size four and two in size two.

"Don't worry, I'll fit her, Marthe," Mr. de la Renta called after them. "Let me just find my measuring tape."

Blair was convinced she was dreaming, so whatever Mr. de la Renta said was fine with her. Marthe helped her into a size two skirt, which fit her like a dream, but as soon as she slipped her arms into the sleeves of the size two jacket, it was clear that the shoulders were going to be too tight. Marthe swapped it for the four, fastened the bow on the narrow leather belt, and then threw open the curtain.

Ta-da!

Blair put her hands on her hips and strutted out of the dressing room like a runway model, swishing the pleated skirt from side to side, a huge grin plastered to her face. Why hadn't she thought of wearing a suit like this before? Not that there *were* many suits like this one. It was elegant and tarty at the same time—totally chic, but most of all, unique.

"Blimey," Marcus breathed. "You're stunning."

And so are you! Blair almost blurted out. Not only was Lord Marcus breathtakingly handsome and royal, he was bosom buddies with the most amazing fashion designer in the universe.

Mr. de la Renta frowned and shook out his measuring

tape. "The waist is all wrong," he fretted, tugging on Blair's jacket. "And the bodice is too high." He undid the belt and unfastened the buttons on the jacket, yanking it roughly away from Blair's arms. "You may keep the skirt, darling. But please, may I make you a jacket that fits?"

May he?

Blair wished Serena or one of her other classmates would walk by and see her standing in the middle of the Oscar de la Renta boutique wearing only her shell pink La Perla bra and one of "Uncle Oscar's" gorgeous pleated skirts, getting fitted for her graduation outfit by Oscar de la Renta *himself*. She glanced at Marcus, who grinned back at her and then silently placed his right hand over his heart, his emerald green eyes shining with adoration.

Whoa.

Blair had to force herself not to pee in her pants. She was so happy, she wasn't sure if she could stand it.

"Hold still," Mr. de la Renta instructed as he lifted her arms and slipped his measuring tape around her 34Bs. Maybe it was the fact that she was surrounded by beautiful men and beautiful clothes, but Blair had the most ridiculous urge to lick his shiny, sexy, bald head. She giggled, wobbling a little in her bare feet as he slid the measuring tape down to measure her hips. "Hold still!"

She squeezed her eyes shut and did her best not to move, truly believing that when she opened them again, she'd find she'd died and gone to heaven.

hey people!

Open call

In case you haven't heard, that weirdo indie film director Ken Mogul has realized no one is ever going to pay much attention to him until he makes a big blockbuster movie, and so he is making one. He's also on a mission to discover the next hot young actress, so he's having an open call for his new feature film, *Breakfast at Fred's*, at the restaurant of the same name in Barneys this Saturday. The movie is a remake of *Breakfast at Tiffany's* with an entirely teenage cast. Guess who's going to be first in line to try out? And guess who absolutely cannot act?

But guess who *can*??!

Hmmm . . . will they choose the girl who definitely knows how to make herself look the part but has no talent, or the girl with talent who doesn't look anything like Audrey Hepburn? Sounds like one of those vacuous catchphrases from *America's Next Top Model*, my all-time favorite love-to-hate-it show.

Prestigious boarding school to expand art curriculum

Aren't I just full of all the latest news? Anyhoo, in case *anyone's* interested, Waverly Prep, a prestigious boarding school in the upper Hudson Valley, is looking for budding young Picassos and Monets. They're expecting a rush of artsy new applicants this fall, but we know of one particular still-schoolless soon-to-be-sophomore who simply can't wait that long. (You don't really want to go to public school, do you, **J**?)

Celebrity body doubles

Britney's got one. Leonardo's got one. And even some of the regulars on New York's society circuit have them. Apparently fashion designer Oscar de la Renta is so much in demand at parties all over the world that he sends his clones to the parties he doesn't care to attend, and to his Madison Avenue boutique to keep the staff on their toes. His body doubles are all relatives of his from the Dominican Republic, and some of them even have his name, so it really isn't a stretch for them to impersonate their famous cousin. Now, if I could just get myself a body double to attend my final exams so I could concentrate on resting up for the parties after graduation!

St. jude's lax coach investigating viagra theft

This warning came in the form of an e-mail, and caught me quite off guard:

Dear Gossip Girl,

Please let your readers know stealing is a serious matter. Whoever took my prescription for Viagra—and I'm pretty sure it was a senior on my lax team—will not graduate! Thank you for your help.

michaels

Any advice on how I should respond?

Sightings

S and **B**, both with huge shopping bags, walking out of **Bergdorf Goodman** and the **Oscar de la Renta** boutique, respectively. Guess they got lucky and found the graduation dresses of their dreams! An unshaven and more-neurotic-than-usual-looking **D** buying a collection of **Pablo Neruda** love poems at **B&N**. Has he gone over the edge this time? Wait, what am I talking about—he always goes over the edge. **V** in the **CVS** in downtown **Williamsburg**, loading up on Jergens antibacterial shower gel. All those prehookup and posthookup showers—gotta be prepared. **J**, with her brother, in the bookstore, reading *The Best Public Schools in NYC*. Has she given up on boarding school already? Hey, **J**—see above. You'd be surprised what can happen in the last few weeks of school. Kids going wild, getting kicked out right and left. You just gotta have faith. It's like that song from *West Side Story*: "There's a place for us! . . ."

I'll stop singing now and pretend to study for my finals.

See you at the open call at Barneys on Saturday morning—who *won't* be there?

You know you love me.

gossip girl

objects reflected in mirror are closer than they appear

"Is this too brown?" Jenny Humphrey asked her sometimes-best friend, Elise Wells. She flicked a tiny Sephora makeup brush over the ridge of her adorable button nose a few times. "I'm trying to reduce the size of my nose."

Like there isn't another part of her body that actually *needs* reducing?

"What nose?" Elise demanded. "You barely even have a nose." Elise had a small nose too, but it was pugged, which was almost worse than having a big honker, because she was tall and was forever concerned that people were staring up at her nose hairs and boogers.

Nose hairs and boogers, oh my!

It was last-period study hall, and Jenny had taken over the kindergarten bathroom, which was always free in the afternoons because the kindergartners went home at two. The stalls were narrower than those in the rest of the bathrooms in the school, and the toilets were only eighteen inches off the ground, with bright pink Hello Kitty toilet seats. Even the sinks were lower, with pink plastic Hello Kitty step stools in front of them and clear pink Hello Kitty soap dispensers. All the Hello Kitty paraphernalia had been donated by a parent from Tokyo who happened to *own* Hello Kitty.

"Have you ever heard of a school called Waverly Prep?" Jenny asked, blotting wine-colored blush onto her lips and then smearing them with Vaseline—another tip she'd learned on TV from some model/actress named Lauren Hutton who was the same age as her dad but was still pretty enough to model for J.Crew.

Elise shook her head. "Is it another boarding school?" She never said it out loud, but Elise hated the idea of Jenny going off to boarding school and leaving her friendless and alone in Constance's tenth grade. Who else would order takeout egg rolls with her and have them delivered right to the blue doors? Who else would tell her—gently—that her shirt would look better *un*tucked?

"Well, I just heard they have this great new art program. Like, they have a real gallery that's open to the public and the students curate the shows and everything. It sounds really cool. Of course, applications were due in, like, December, but I was thinking maybe I could send them some of my artwork. . ." Jenny zipped up her yellow-and-pink striped LeSportsac makeup bag, watching herself in one of the diminutive, square over-the-sink mirrors as she talked. Lauren Hutton was right. Her nose did look smaller. If only her dark hair weren't so darned curly and unmanageable. "This is my last chance. If I don't get in there, I'm going to have to go to public school."

Heaven forbid!

"I just wish I hadn't burned all those paintings . . ." she added wistfully and rubbed her lips together one last time.

Back when she'd been in love with Nate, Jenny had painted his portrait in the style of each of her favorite painters: Matisse, Picasso, Chagall, Monet, Warhol, Pollock. The paintings had been vivid and full of emotion, as if she'd been trying to invoke love itself right there on the canvas. But when Nate had broken her heart, she'd set fire to them in a metal trash can out on the sidewalk in front of her building, burning every last one.

Elise bared her teeth at the mirror, trying to dig out the remains of the orange she'd eaten for lunch with her jagged, unpainted pinky nail. "Yeah, but would you really want to send a boarding school a whole bunch of paintings of some boy you don't even talk to anymore?" she asked reasonably.

Well, at least they'd know I was capable of having *a boyfriend,* Jenny retorted silently, suddenly irked by the preppiness of Elise's shell pink Peter Pan–collared blouse and the way her breath always smelled like yesterday's egg rolls.

Besides, Waverly sounded like the kind of school that was always evolving; not a party school per se, but a school that wasn't afraid to try something new or take a risk on someone.

Like *her*, for instance?

Elise stopped picking her teeth and reached for Jenny's makeup bag, opening it without asking permission and unscrewing a tube of shimmering lilac-colored Stila lip gloss. She puckered her wide mouth and began generously smearing lip gloss all over it.

When Jenny really thought about it, she had taken a risk on Elise. First she had been friendless, and now she had a friend, whether she liked it or not.

"You're right," she mused, retrieving her makeup bag and spilling it into one of the small, low sinks. "I should send Waverly something new anyway. Something I haven't tried before." She sorted through the assortment of eyeliners, shadows, and glosses, looking for her favorite Clinique four-shades-of-gray eye shadow palette in its mint green plastic case. "Would you mind if I painted your portrait with this?" she asked her friend, holding up the palette and feeling suddenly inspired. She'd do Elise in eye shadow, her dad in red wine, and Dan in . . . instant coffee. It was innovative and meaningful, and way better than sending Waverly a tear sheet of her jog bra modeling debut or her first appearance on Page Six.

Not that Jenny wasn't still a party girl looking for a party school, but Serena van der Woodsen had taught her a very important lesson: Party girls are deeper and smarter than they first appear.

be still her cheating heart

Vanessa was sitting on the floor in her living room wearing only the black SUGARDADDY DID HUNGARY T-shirt her sister, Ruby, had sent her from Budapest, a recent stop on her band's tour, and a pair of somebody's gray-and-white striped boxers—it was getting hard to keep them straight. She was trying to smoothly splice together Chuck Bass's horrifying and amusing interview, complete with pet snow monkey, with Kati and Isabel talking about how they'd decided to go to Rollins College in Florida together even though Isabel had gotten into Princeton. Chuck was wearing a tight white wifebeater T-shirt and was rubbing his beefy, unnaturally tan arms with Bain de Soleil dark tanning oil as he explained how he stayed golden brown all year. His monkey remained curled in his lap, blinking stupidly at the camera with its creepy light blue eyes.

"Normally I lie in the beds like once, maybe twice a week, or I use this amazing Estée Lauder bronzing stuff to keep it nice and even all year round. I wonder, though—do you happen to know if there's a good tanning salon near Fort Lee?"

Isabel and Kati were lying on their backs with their heads pressed together—Isabel's sleek and dark and Kati's frizzy and strawberry blond—smiling up at the camera like sisters who looked nothing alike.

"It's like, how am I going to concentrate in, like, Intro to Law at Princeton, if my best friend in the whole world is down in Florida all by herself?" Isabel demanded gaily, her lips so thoroughly glossed, they were practically dripping.

"Besides, we're both going to lose ten pounds this summer on the South Beach Diet so we can look awesome in our matching Shoshanna black-and-red paisley bikinis, which we get to wear every single day!" Kati shrieked excitedly, kicking her bare legs so hard, her light-blue-and-white seersucker uniform flipped up, revealing her sensible white cotton Gap underwear.

The crazy thing was that the more Vanessa replayed the interviews, the more she realized she was actually going to miss these people, freak shows that they were, and she wondered for their sake if there was any way to make them sound more intelligent and less insane.

Probably not. And what would be the fun of that anyway?

As she worked, she couldn't help feeling distracted by the knowledge that just over the Williamsburg Bridge, the indie film director Ken Mogul was casting his first moneymaking blockbuster venture, *Breakfast at Fred's*, which would be filmed at Fred's restaurant in Barneys department store on Sixtieth and Madison. Months before, Ken Mogul had spotted a piece of Vanessa's film footage that had accidentally been leaked on the Internet and tried to hire her to work with him. He'd wanted her to quit school and postpone college. Of course, Vanessa had said no. But now Ken Mogul was in New York, making a movie right under her nose. She was supposed to be driving around the country with Aaron this summer anyway, but . . .

It's kind of tempting, huh?

Someone knocked on the front door. "Yeah?" Vanessa called out before getting up to see who it was. Aaron was supposed to come over after band practice and had promised to bring Thai food for dinner and help her study for her math exam. He was due any minute, but he had a key. She got up and peered through the little glass peephole in the door. There was no one there.

Hearing faint footsteps echoing on the stairs, she shifted her gaze and squinted, just making out Dan's skinny, navy-blue-board-shorts-clad ass as it disappeared up the grubby black steps on his way to the roof. She'd forgotten he still had a key, too.

Already Vanessa could feel the adrenaline rush she'd felt the last time Dan had come over. Was it being with him that made her feel this way, or was it the notion that Aaron could walk through the door at any moment and catch them? Did it even matter?

Hell no.

She scribbled a hasty note to Aaron—*Went to get laundry*—even though she'd already picked up her laundry at the Wash 'n' Fold that morning before school. Then she threw open the front door and dashed upstairs.

Dan was lying on his back on the futon underneath the water tower, wearing only his black cotton boxer briefs, leafing through a glossy-pink-covered collection of Pablo Neruda love poems. Beside him on a tinfoil tray were four bluepoint oysters from Zabar's and an open bottle of red Merlot with two Styrofoam cups. When he saw Vanessa, he immediately sat up and began to read aloud.

Don't go far off, not even for a day, because—
Because—I don't know how to say it: a day is long.

"Do you think maybe you could call first before you come over?" Vanessa demanded, pretending to be furious, because she knew it turned Dan on to see her mad. "Aaron's coming over, like, right now."

"That's from a poem called 'I Crave Your Mouth, Your Voice, Your Hair,'" Dan explained, gazing at her sweetly. He poured a little wine into a cup and held it out. "Want some?"

Vanessa rolled her eyes and went over to the futon. "I think I know what you crave." She sat down and took off her shirt, the adrenaline pumping even harder now. "Hurry up," she ordered. "Aaron's bringing my dinner and then I have studying to do."

Neighbors in the surrounding apartments adjusted their telescopes. They'd moved to the area because the rent was cheap. Who knew there was also going to be built-in, live entertainment?!

The bossier and pissier Vanessa was, the more hot and bothered Dan grew, and the more he loved her. His hands shook and sweat formed on his freshly shaved upper lip. He was entirely at her mercy.

Down on Broadway, Aaron ignored the group of bystanders on the other side of the street, all staring up at the roof of Vanessa's building. He was carrying two orders of hot and spicy pad Thai in a paper bag under his arm, he had to pee, the freaking L train was insanely crowded, and he was sweating his ass off. All he wanted was to get inside and take a nice cool shower. Preferably with Vanessa.

He found her note and scribbled over it, *I'm in the tub.* Then he left the front door standing open to make it easier for her to bring her basket of clean laundry inside and turned on the stereo, blasting that Raves song Dan Humphrey had recorded with them—the only one that was any good.

"Crack me like an egg!" Aaron sang along in the shower.

Three floors up, Dan was already ramming his feet back into his socks. The music was faint but unmistakable.

"Do you think he saw us?" A little thrill ran through Vanessa's body at the thought. God, was she perverse!

Dan hastily slurped down the last oyster. "What do you want me to do?" he asked, sounding just as excited as she did. *See how perfect we are for each other?* he thought. They were both totally getting off on the fact that Aaron had no clue. Of course, cheating was bad and wrong, but it was totally fun when you were completely, madly in love with the person you were doing it with!

"I'll go downstairs and distract him," Vanessa whispered, even though the traffic on the Williamsburg Bridge was so loud no one could possibly have heard her. "While you leave."

Dan shoved the cork into the half-drunk bottle of Merlot and tried to prop it up inside his black Manhattan Transfer messenger bag. "You want me to leave?" he responded, baffled. He'd imagined scaling the outside of the building like Spider-Man with Vanessa clinging to his neck like Kirsten Dunst.

Like that would ever happen, Mr. Spaghetti Arms.

"You can leave that here." Vanessa pointed at the wine. "We'll drink it later."

We meaning she and Dan, or she and Aaron?

"Fine," Dan replied, catching on to the fact that Vanessa was about to go downstairs and pretend he'd never even been there. God, she was smart. And so tough and cool under pressure. "Good luck studying this weekend."

Vanessa gave his butt a little slap. "I'll call you," she promised before hurrying downstairs. The door to the apartment was open and Aaron was in the shower.

Vanessa undressed for the second time in fifteen minutes.

"Hi," she greeted him, yanking back the shower curtain.

"Hey." Aaron grinned and held out a soap-flecked hand to help her in.

Dan tiptoed slowly downstairs, reading Neruda aloud to himself, his hands sweating as he tried to figure out if what had just happened was either insanely exciting or insanely insulting.

. . . In this part of the story I am the one who dies . . .

The problem with poets like him is they always err on the negative side.

guess who's coming to breakfast at fred's?

Saturday morning, the line of gorgeous girls wound its way out Barneys' front doors, up Madison to Sixty-first Street, and around the corner to Fifth Avenue. Most of them were wearing black sleeveless cocktail dresses, pointy black flats, and black Jackie Onassis-big sunglasses. Serena was wearing her favorite new pair of True Religion jeans.

Typical.

Somehow, she'd managed to be one of the first girls in line. Maybe it was because she and Nate had never really gone to sleep last night—thanks to the little bottle of pills he kept popping?—and she'd still been awake at five A.M. She'd just grabbed a double latte at the deli and headed over, lugging her French textbook with her, as if she'd really get any studying done.

Blair *was* first in line. And, surprise, surprise, she *was* Audrey Hepburn. Same black vintage Givenchy dress, same pearl choker, same French-twist hairstyle—with the help of a little faux hair—same oversize Chanel sunglasses, same black elbow-length gloves. Lord Marcus, being the sweet and charming hunk that he was, had helped her get dressed and even had come up with the idea of spending the night in a hired town car, parked right in front of Barneys, so she'd be sure to be first in line for the open call. Of course, they hadn't been able to do much for fear of messing up her costume, but it was still fun to hold hands in the backseat and talk about the very near future, when Blair would be a famous Hollywood star.

"I'll be your pool lad," Lord Marcus offered in his adorable English accent. "I'll fan you with palm fronds and pour your cocktails." Of course he wouldn't mind giving up his spot in the graduate business program at the London School of Economics, where he was starting in the fall. He'd do anything for Blair—anything!

"And I'll have the best designers making clothes for me in every city in the world," Blair fantasized over her stomach's nervous rumblings. She wanted this part so badly, she hadn't eaten all day, but it was nearly midnight and she was famished. "Or maybe I'll ask Uncle Oscar to make all my clothes."

A hot dog vendor was packing up for the night on the corner of Sixty-first and Madison. Would Lord Marcus be perfectly horrified if she ate one, standing on the curb in front of Barneys?

It would be no worse than Audrey Hepburn eating a Danish out of a paper bag in front of Tiffany's.

"Look, darling, dinner!" Lord Marcus cried, noticing the vendor and literally reading Blair's mind. "You sit tight and I'll go fetch us some."

Darling. She was his darling, and he fetched things for her!

So they'd eaten Sabrett hot dogs with mustard and relish and sipped A&W root beer, holding hands and dozing off until Blair's eyelids had fluttered open to find Serena looming out of the early morning mist in her perfectly distressed jeans and no makeup. She'd bolted out of the car and slapped her black Chanel sunglasses over her eyes. No way was that blond bitch going to steal her part in this show.

Never mind the other hundreds of actress-wannabes who were beginning to turn up for the audition.

Now it was nearly eight o'clock and the audition was about

to begin. It was an unusually hot and humid May morning and the two girls stood front-to-back at the head of the line, fanning themselves with the page of lines Ken Mogul's helpers had handed out and which they'd already memorized.

Finally Serena could stand it no longer. "God, it's hot." Blair didn't respond, so Serena reached out and touched Blair's bare arm. "So, that guy you've been hanging out with—he seems really nice," she ventured awkwardly.

Blair wished she were taller so she could gaze down at Serena with such hawklike severity that Serena would never attempt to speak to her again. Alas, she was nearly six inches shorter than Serena, especially since she was wearing the required Holly Golightly-esque superflat flats.

She was about to give a short and extremely nasty reply when she realized something startling. She didn't even mind anymore that Serena had Nate. She had the hotter, taller, more refined, better-bred, British version of Nate, and she was perfectly happy with him, thank you very much. In fact, just to prove how fine she was with everything, they could all be friends—the four of them.

She pushed her enormous Chanel sunglasses on top of her head and smiled brightly up at her former friend. "How about after this the four of us all get a drink down at the Yale Club together? They have a great lounge. It's like a hotel bar out of an old movie or something. You'd love it."

"*Really?*" Serena gasped, wondering if she might be dreaming. Had Blair really just invited her and Nate to have a drink with her and her new boyfriend?

"Sorry for the wait, ladies. All right, Blair Waldorf, you're up," announced a skinny guy in his twenties with a hipster-mullet haircut and faded Diesel jeans rolled up to his knees.

Blair flipped her sunglasses back onto her nose.

"Good luck," Serena said faintly, still unsure of whether they were really talking to each other or not.

Mullet guy led Blair inside the store—thank goodness for

air-conditioning!—and across the cosmetics floor to the elevators. Barneys didn't open until ten on Saturdays, so it was weirdly quiet. Of course, Blair spent so much time there, she could have found her way to Fred's blindfolded, but that wasn't enough to get her the part.

Fred's, the store's notorious restaurant, was up on the ninth floor. Long and narrow, with windows along one wall overlooking Madison, and a small, modern bar, it was the type of restaurant that was surprisingly unspectacular looking given its popularity. What made it spectacular was its usual clientele—the Holly Golightlys of the present day and their Park-Avenue-dwelling mothers or publicists, all dressed in Chanel and Prada, sipping white wine spritzers and picking at their salads while they worried about whether someone else was going to buy the last pair of faun-colored Costume National knee-high stiletto boots they had spotted on their way up to the restaurant.

Right now, though, the restaurant was empty, except for Ken Mogul and his crew. The director was standing by the bar giving lighting direction to a gaggle of Swedish-looking blond female crewpeople in matching black tunics, his notorious bulging blue eyes bloodshot with fatigue. He sported a short, prickly, reddish beard with no mustache—never a good look—and shoulder-length curly red hair. His 1980s-style leather jacket had huge rounded shoulders, and his Levi's were way too tight—also not a good look. Blair had never seen him before and thought he might be one of the crew until he addressed her.

"Well, you certainly *look* the part." He pointed to one of the chrome-and-black-leather bar stools, gesturing for her to sit down. "But this isn't a complete remake, you know. I'm taking some liberties. For instance, Holly might not have brown hair. And she could be tall."

Way to rub a brunette who's always been on the shorter side the wrong way!

It had taken Blair three hours to get dressed, so she decided to ignore his insult. She folded up the sheet of paper she'd been given to read from and tucked it into her purse, partly to impress Ken Mogul with the fact that she'd already memorized her lines, and partly to show that her feathers weren't easily ruffled. Then she sat down on a bar stool and crossed her legs with Audrey Hepburn-like balletic grace.

"I'm not going to give you any direction," Ken Mogul remarked. "You just do your thing, okay? So . . . action!"

Blair had Googled Ken Mogul and found a ton of articles about how he called himself the "*un*director," and how actors hated working with him because he just stared at them without giving them any direction at all. He probably thought he was terribly avant-garde or whatever. Well, that was fine with her, because she didn't need any direction—she *was* Audrey Hepburn playing Holly Golightly twenty-four hours a day.

She pulled a cigarette and the long ebony-and-mother-of-pearl cigarette holder she'd found in an antique shop in Rhode Island two summers ago out of her slim black satin vintage Chanel pocketbook.

"*How* do you *do*?" she purred, sounding exactly like Audrey at her most charming. She lit her cigarette and blew a delicate stream of smoke over Ken Mogul's head. Then she delivered that dreamy, faraway smile that was Audrey's trademark. "Don't you just *love* it here? Isn't it *wonderful* waking up and knowing this place is *right here*, every day? It's my absolute *paradise*."

Blair waited for Ken Mogul's response. Those were the only lines she'd been given to say, and she'd said them perfectly, even if she did say so herself.

Ken Mogul covered his bulging blue eyes with his hand and then pulled it roughly away again in a bizarre game of peekaboo. He stared at Blair for a moment longer and then yelled, "Next!"

Blair dropped down off the stool and walked gracefully

out of the restaurant to where Lord Marcus was waiting for her near the elevator doors. He gathered her in his strong, capable, royal arms. "You were stunning," he reassured her. "I was watching from the door."

Blair leaned her cheek against his chest, still in character. "I do love it here," she sighed dreamily.

The elevator doors rolled open and Serena and Nate stepped out.

"Good luck!" Blair called out generously. She took another drag on her cigarette holder and offered Nate a serene smile. He smiled weakly back at her, looking a little red around the eyes, like he'd been crying, or, more likely, was extremely stoned. But from where Blair stood, with her body pressed against her hunky British lord, that was really none of her concern.

Then Lord Marcus kissed the back of Blair's head, sending a little thrill down her spine. The door to the ladies' lounge was right in front of them. She took his hand and tugged him toward it.

Nothing better than a little make-out session before breakfast.

s gets to say her lines twice

Serena worried that she should have dressed up like the other girls. Would the director think she wasn't trying hard enough because she hadn't worn pearls and a black cocktail dress? Plus, she was blond and big-boned and tall and didn't look a thing like Audrey Hepburn. In fact, now that she thought about it, she really shouldn't have been trying out for the part at all.

Too late.

"Oh, thank God," Ken Mogul exclaimed when he saw her. "Go ahead. *Action.*"

Serena hadn't bothered to Google Ken Mogul, and she didn't know anything about his directing style, but she knew what the word *action* meant, and the minute she heard it, she started to do her thing.

"How do you do?" she chirped brightly, holding her hand out to an imaginary bartender. She took a seat and then spun once around on the bar stool, giggling and kicking her feet with girlish satisfaction. "Don't you just love it here? Isn't it wonderful waking up and knowing this place is right here, every day? It's my absolute paradise!"

Ken Mogul did that weird peekaboo thing with his hands again. He glanced at one of his Swedish-looking blond crew girls, ripped off the pair of mirrored aviator shades she had propped on her head, and tossed them to Serena.

"Do it again with these on," he ordered.

Serena did as she was told, wondering if it was a good thing or a bad thing that Ken Mogul closed his eyes when she started to talk.

"Next!" he shouted, dismissing her.

Nate was standing by the elevators, a damp tissue wadded in his fist. "My mom brought me here to buy my first real suit," he told Serena, his lower lip trembling. "Afterwards we got ice cream and she took me to the zoo in the park. It smelled like peanuts."

"Aw." Serena hugged him and kissed his ear. "Listen, I think I know of a way to cheer you up." After the Viagra incident in Bergdorf's on Tuesday, Serena thought Nate was basically up for it any time, anywhere. She nodded toward the ladies' lounge.

Nate hesitated. He'd smoked a tiny joint when he woke up, and he'd left the Viagra at home. Besides, all this crying was so exhausting. He really wasn't in the mood.

The ladies' lounge door swung open, and Blair and that sandy-haired hunk of hers came out, holding hands. "How do you do?" Blair gestured with her empty cigarette holder in an exaggerated imitation of the part both girls had just played. She giggled. "You guys want to go get a drink?"

"Definitely," Serena gushed eagerly.

Of course, it was only ten-thirty on a Saturday morning, but the future Audreys of the world clearly know how to enjoy themselves.

Lord Marcus pressed the button for the elevator and the doors rolled open.

"Wait!" one of Ken Mogul's black-tunic-wearing, blond crew girls yelled. Blair's heart skipped a beat. Surely they were going to offer her the part right now and send the other girls packing. But the girl was looking at Serena.

"Oops!" Serena blushed, swiping the mirrored aviators off her head and handing them back. "I'm such a klepto!"

The girl took the sunglasses and then stood on tiptoe to whisper in Serena's ear. Blair watched, riveted, as Serena nodded, listening silently. Then the crew girl left to supply her sunglasses to another Holly hopeful.

Blair bit her lip, nearly drawing blood. The need to know what the crewperson had whispered to Serena was killing her, but she forced herself not to ask, and Serena decided not to tell her. The idea that they were sort of talking to each other again was so tenuous and so new, neither of them wanted to ruin it.

Plus, Lord Marcus had only seen Blair on her best behavior. She couldn't pull an *Exorcist* and freak out in front of him now or he'd pack his bags and head back to the U.K. as quick as you can say, "Bloody hell."

Serena reached for Nate's hand and gave it an excited squeeze, barely able to keep the secret to herself. "Let's go get silly."

"Hear, hear!" Lord Marcus agreed.

Blair didn't even flinch at the sight of Serena and Nate holding hands. She'd always wanted to be a foursome; she'd just always thought it would be her and Nate and Serena and someone else. She looked up into Lord Marcus's handsome golf-course-green eyes and he swooped down and kissed her tenderly on the tip of her nose.

Nate had never been that into public displays of affection. And anyway, what had ever been so special about Nate?

boys will be boys and girls will be girls

"I heard about you. You're the kid who's to take my place on the Yale lacrosse team. Excuse me, ladies." Lord Marcus reached across Blair and Serena to clasp Nate's hand in the cramped backseat of the cab as it raced down the hot Park Avenue blacktop. "Coach said you were a maniac with a stick."

That's one way of putting it.

Nate hoped Lord Marcus wouldn't guess that he'd been crying. Now would've been a good time to take another Viagra, just to give him an ego boost and keep the tears from flowing. If it hadn't been for those annoying side effects, he'd have taken it every day.

What, like the major hard-ons? But that's not a side effect, that's the whole point!

"So is Yale, like, seriously tough or what?" Nate asked, because it was the only thing he could think of to say. Blair had her head on Lord Marcus's shoulder, and she looked so comfortable, it was sort of unsettling and nice to see at the same time. Her dark hair was growing out and it looked so soft and shiny, Nate could almost feel it in his hands.

Oh, please. Don't cry.

"Not as hard as Coach Heffner's arse," Lord Marcus joked. "She told us all about how she stabbed you with a fork when you tried to hit on her."

Nate had pretty much blocked that little episode out of his mind, and he flinched, remembering. "I just wasn't expecting a hot female coach," he admitted.

"Believe me, none of us were," Lord Marcus replied with a knowing smile. He lit a Marlboro Red, but the tiny, shriveled cabdriver flapped his hand in annoyance, so he threw it out the window.

"Let's all light cigarettes and see what he does," Serena whispered, still feeling giddy. She handed out four Merit Ultra Lights from her black suede Balenciaga fringed hobo bag and Lord Marcus helped her light them with a silver Tiffany lighter.

The driver screeched to a halt when he noticed the smoke. "Get out of my cab!" he shouted, his tiny, shriveled fists raised in anger.

Lord Marcus, ever the polite Englishman, began to apologize, pretending he didn't know it was illegal to smoke in American taxis. But they were already on Park Avenue and Forty-seventh Street, just around the corner from the Yale Club, so they got out anyway.

What a sight: a lovely brunette dressed exactly like Audrey Hepburn in *Breakfast at Tiffany's*, two handsome, green-eyed, lacrosse-playing, neatly dressed boys, and a heart-wrenchingly gorgeous blonde in jeans. The Yale Club's dress code forbade distressed denim, but Serena looked so pretty in her jeans, no one cared. As soon as they stepped into the club's sparse, neoclassical lobby, all the middle-aged Yale alums in J. Press suits stopped talking business and switched off their BlackBerrys. Oh, to be seventeen and irresistible!

As if any of them were ever this irresistible.

Lord Marcus took Nate up to his suite to show him some lacrosse trophy that only Nate would appreciate, while Blair led Serena into the club's lounge, where they settled in at the elegant bar with its gold ceiling, polished wood floor, and dark wood paneling. Of course they were used to going out all the time, but it still felt extremely grown-up to be out at a private club bar on a Saturday morning, especially when they were supposed to be glued to their textbooks, studying for their final exams, which would begin on Monday.

"So, what are you going to say in your graduation speech?" Serena asked Blair. "What's that Dr. Seuss book—you know the one everyone always quotes from?"

Blair rolled her eyes. She was so *not* quoting from that book. "*Oh, The Places You'll Go!*"

The bow-tied bartender brought Blair's drink first—a Ketel One martini straight up with an olive. She took a sip and then stuck a cigarette into her cigarette holder. She was enjoying the whole cigarette holder thing so much, she planned to use it right up until *Breakfast at Fred's* came out and all the girls started copying her.

Ergo, the difference between being trendy and being a trendsetter.

"Actually, I'm going to write about going after what you want and getting it," she declared, blowing smoke over the top of Serena's pale blond head. "I never thought I'd get absolutely everything I wanted. But I kept trying, anyway, and now I have it. *Everything.*"

Serena nodded. "I know what you mean." The bartender brought her Tanqueray gin fizz and she took a few tentative sips, wondering if she should tell Blair right now that when Ken Mogul's assistant had whispered in her ear, she'd asked Serena back for a second audition. But things were going so well with Blair at the moment, she didn't want to ruin it. Besides, even if she wound up being offered the part, she wasn't sure she wanted it. She tried to think of something else to say, something about getting what she'd always wanted, even though she'd never really wanted anything— things just fell into her lap.

"I'm so in love with Nate," she blurted out, trying to sound as thrilled with the way things had turned out as Blair did.

Blair lit the end of her cigarette. How easy it would be to accidentally set fire to Serena's long black eyelashes. She surveyed the room, trying to decide whether or not to let her temper get the better of her.

Whoa, she's *thinking* about it? Is this a turning point?!

Blair loved the Yale Club lounge. The gold-leaf paint and oriental carpets made it feel grand and exclusive, but it was more comfortable and less stodgy than some of the other rooms in the club. The lounge was the perfect place to escape from the heat. And it went with her dress. "Pretty soon we'll all be at Yale," she mused.

The two girls stared at each other, their blue eyes locked, trying to decide whether that was a good thing or a bad thing.

Serena giggled. "And we can take the train back to the city and stay here, and our parents won't even know we're in town!"

That does sound like fun.

"This would be such a great place to have a party," Blair chimed in, deciding to be nice. She blinked, wondering why she hadn't thought of it before. Of course, it meant there'd be a lot of random crashers—other seniors from dopey schools that she didn't even know, and random juniors who thought they were cool now because they were going to be seniors next year. But she was Constance Billard's graduation speaker. It made perfect sense that she should host a graduation party—*the* graduation party.

She gave Serena a stiff hug, barely keeping her cigarette holder aloft to avoid setting fire to her hair. "We always have the best ideas," she murmured, half to herself and half to her old friend.

Serena smiled eagerly, even though she had no idea which ideas Blair was referring to. "Don't we?" she agreed.

Nate had brought a couple of prerolled joints along with him. He and Lord Marcus made themselves comfortable in the lord's gold-and-white-wallpapered suite, blasting the AC as they lay on their backs on the king-size, apricot-colored bedspread, puffing away and trading secrets about Blair.

See, boys really are worse than girls.

"She acts all grumpy when you come on to her, and then she complains when you don't," Nate complained, shaking his head. "I never understood that."

"But as long as you let her know she's irresistible, she can't make a fuss," Lord Marcus pointed out. "That's what's crucial."

Nate turned his head to look at the older boy through a haze of pot smoke. He'd known Blair practically since he was born. How come this guy, who'd only just met her, seemed to have her all figured out? Was it possible that he and Blair were totally incompatible? Maybe they were actually never meant to be.

Nate couldn't think about it anymore without having a major sob attack. Instead, he took another hit and allowed his mind to go heavenly blank.

"I'm thinking of asking Blair to come over to England to visit for the summer," Lord Marcus mused aloud. "I've told my family all about her and they're desperate to meet her. Apparently my dad knows her dad. And my mum's already got us married off."

Nate took another hit. No need to get upset. His mind was as smooth, white, and wrinkle-free as the 800-thread-count pillow shams on Lord Marcus's bed.

Lord Marcus finished off his joint and sat up, stubbing it out neatly on the sole of his amber-colored Tod's lace-ups. "The ladies will be wondering where we are." He clapped Nate on the shoulder. "Shall we go, then?"

Nate sat up on his elbows and shook his head blearily, like a dog. A stray tear seeped out of the corner of his left eye and trickled down his cheek. He swatted it away angrily, but then another one began to trickle out of the corner of his right eye.

"Are you all right?" Lord Marcus asked. "Do you need a minute?"

Nate shrugged, and then his lower lip began to tremble.

Lord Marcus sat down next to him and pulled Nate into his arms. "There, there," he murmured. "You're all right."

This wasn't the pretend gay affection that Nate and his friends used to drive one another nuts. This was the real thing: a big-brotherly hug. Nate had never had a big brother, or any siblings for that matter, and the hug was exactly what he needed.

"*Mon père habite en France dans le Loire. Il aime des autres hommes. Il est un fag!*" Blair shrieked, and she and Serena burst into a fit of giggles.

"*Qu'est-ce que vous faites, mes chéries?*" Lord Marcus called out as he and Nate approached.

"We're conversing in French. There's an oral part to my AP exam. We have to talk about our family for ten minutes," Blair explained. "Using all the tenses."

Serena rolled her eyes. "That's what you get for taking APs." She squinted at the two boys. "Hey, are you two stoned?"

Nate grinned sheepishly. "Slightly."

"You big idiot." Serena grabbed him and kissed him smack on the lips, bubbling over with relief that she and Blair were talking again.

Blair was so fine with seeing Serena and Nate kiss right in front of her, she didn't budge. Within seconds Lord Marcus had slipped behind her and wrapped his arms sexily around her waist—the sort of husbandlike, proprietary gesture Blair had always dreamed about. He winked at Serena. "Did you know *Serena* means *mermaid* in Italian?"

"Yeah," Serena giggled and then flashed Blair a look that said, *Where'd you find him, anyway?*

Blair returned the look with a smug smile that was a combination of *See, I told you I had everything* and *Hands off, bitchface.*

Nate licked the taste of Serena's vanilla-scented MAC lip

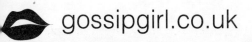 gossipgirl.co.uk

Disclaimer: All the real names of places, people, and events have been altered or abbreviated to protect the innocent. Namely, me.

hey people!

A not-so-private party at the yale club

In case you were feeling left out of Saturday's Yale Club all-day-and-all-night festival of debauchery—they certainly kept the staff busy trotting over to Grand Central for more Prosecco from the Campbell Apartment and cheesecake from Junior's—a certain Yalie-to-be will host the graduation party of a lifetime at the club next Monday night. The Yale Club is strictly members-only, but never fear. Yalie Daddy has paid the club handsomely to keep its doors open all night long to any well-dressed merrymaker who wanders in looking for more ways to make merry. It's his way of apologizing to his daughter for not being there in the flesh. Aw, how sweet.

Let's hope he doesn't forget that she will also need some way of getting around New Haven next year. Vroom, vroom.

Postbreakfast depression

Ken Mogul is either extremely fussy, extremely mean, or both. Rumor has it that only four girls were called back for a second audition for the lead role in his new feature film, *Breakfast at Fred's*. Another rumor is that he's casting his younger sister in the Holly Golightly part and the casting on Saturday was actually just for extras. What a waste of talent.

An arranged marriage

We've all heard about how the British royals have a penchant for arranged marriages. It saves a lot of trouble and embarrassment when no one has to sneak around or worry about introducing their socially inept, badly dressed girlfriend to their mom, who happens to be the queen. Well, according to my sources in the U.K., a certain blue-blooded English hunk, who recently graduated from Yale and is currently residing at the Yale Club while he finishes up some business—aka partying—in New York before going home for the summer, has been betrothed to an equally royal English girl since he was barely two years old. I haven't seen a picture of her, but having witnessed how quickly he snapped up our **B**, my guess is she's probably not much of a looker, and he's probably not too thrilled about marrying her.

Thief of stolen goods identified

Not that I want to be the bearer of more bad news, but my coach friend has been e-mailing me regularly—hey, who gave him this link?!—and apparently the Viagra perp has been identified and will be punished accordingly. Does that mean he/she won't graduate??

Your e-mail

Dear GG,
I know I shouldn't have, but I kind of told on one of my pals and now I'm worried he's not gonna graduate cuz of me. I just thought, better him than me, you know?
—lamo

Dear lamo,
Yeah, that *was* kind of lamo. But you know that already.
—GG

Dear Gossip Girl,
I wanted to personally invite you to try out for my new movie. You have the attitude I'm looking for. Hopefully you have the look. When r u available?
—mogs

 Dear mogs,
Nice try.
—GG

Sightings

B, S, N, and **Lord M** at **Cipriani Dolci** across from the **Yale Club,** drinking Bloody Marys at Sunday brunch. They certainly know how to prepare for finals! **V** with **A** in his red **Saab,** pretending not to notice when they almost ran over **D** crossing Houston Street on their way to a movie at the **Angelika. D** was on his way back from one of those Chinese herbalists on Canal Street, carrying a small pouch of what was advertised as "Love Potion XXX." Oh, the tangled web we weave. **J** alone in the Gristedes on West Ninety-sixth Street buying a liter screw-top bottle of red wine and a jumbo-size can of Folgers instant crystals. Her clothes and hands were smeared with what looked like gray eye shadow, coffee, and wine. Obviously, she's so dedicated to her art, they didn't dare card her.

One more week to go

So this is it, my sweetnesses—the final stretch. Aside from exams, which are just trivial annoyances really, school is essentially over. Repeat after me: only one week till graduation. Only one week till graduation. Only one week till graduation.

Good luck!!!!

You know you love me.

gossip girl

d writes another ode

Dan finished his AP English exam with twenty minutes to spare and began rewriting his graduation speech about love in the back of his blue book. This time he planned on quoting from Robert Frost's poem "The Road Not Taken":

Two roads diverged in a wood, and I—
I took the one less traveled by,
And that has made all the difference.

The words sounded sterile and entirely overused to him, though, especially in the context of graduation. Besides, neither he nor his classmates were actually taking the road less traveled. They were graduating and going straight to college. And how boring was that? The truth was, it had never really occurred to him to do anything else. Until now.

He'd been battling with the notion for days that come fall, Vanessa would be here in New York and he would be there, in Olympia, Washington—on the other side of the country. The thought was unbearable to him, even though he was still unsure of Vanessa's true feelings for him, especially after she'd so brusquely dismissed him the other night the minute Aaron had come home and had proceeded to not call him all weekend.

But maybe he was the one who hadn't been clear. He'd already told that nutty professor he'd decided not to spend the summer working in Olympia. Why not take it one step further and announce to everyone at graduation that he wasn't going to college, period. That would show Vanessa, and the world, how far he was willing to go—for love. He would take the road less traveled by.

Dan turned the page and scribbled the words *Ode on Love*, modeling his new poem on those of his favorite poet, John Keats. Keats wrote odes all the time: "Ode to Psyche," "Ode on a Grecian Urn," "Ode to a Nightingale," "Ode on Melancholy," but never an "Ode on Love." So why shouldn't Dan be the one to do it?

"Seventeen minutes to go," Ms. Solomon called out. Dan glanced up at the stiff backs of his classmates bent over their desks, pens working frantically as the black wall clock ticked the minutes by. He went back to his blue book. "Ode on Love." Of course, his love for Vanessa was mixed with a heavy dose of undying lust. But how to convey that without sounding pornographic? After all, the poem was supposed to be part of his graduation speech.

Your milky white orbs,
The pillows of your stomach,
Thighs like birches.

Ew, enough!!

He drew a heavy *X* across the words. *The pillows of your stomach?* Yuck.

Exactly.

Then he remembered the lines from "Ode on a Grecian Urn":

More happy love! more happy, happy love!
Forever warm and still to be enjoyed

Forever panting, and forever young;
All breathing human passion far above,
That leaves a heart high-sorrowful and cloyed,
A burning forehead and a parching tongue.

Was there any better way to say it?

Probably not.

Dan began to sketch a picture of the water tower on top of Vanessa's building, but he was no artist and his water tower looked more like a giant acorn. If only he were allowed to use his phone during exams. He could call the Evergreen admissions office and let them know he wasn't coming.

Instead, he tried to rework the opening segment of his graduation speech in the last few pages of his blue book.

Ladies and gentlemen, thank you for attending this year's commencement exercises for the Riverside Preparatory School for Boys. You must be very proud of your sons—so proud that you are giving them exactly what they wanted for graduation, right? (Pause for laughter.)

Anyway, I'm honored to be the graduation speaker this year. I'd like to start out by reading from a Robert Frost poem.

Two roads diverged in a wood, and I—
I took the one less traveled by,
And that has made all the difference.

This is a popular quote for graduation speeches. I know, because I Googled it. (Pause for laughter.) *It's ironic, though, because how many of us are actually taking the road less traveled?* (Pause for awkward silence.) *Well, I am. And here's how I'm going to do it: I'm going to follow my heart—*

The little white egg-shaped egg timer on Ms. Solomon's desk went off. "Put down your pencils, please," she announced.

Dan looked up with a dazed expression. As usual, he'd gotten carried away.

"Didn't finish the exam, huh?" Chuck Bass snickered to his left. Seniors were allowed to break dress code for exams, and Chuck had chosen to wear a bright yellow cut-up Dolce & Gabbana sleeveless shirt that was somehow more revealing than if he hadn't worn a shirt at all.

Dan glared at him. Was it possible to be killed in the line of duty while you were still only in military school? He certainly hoped so.

Ms. Solomon walked over to collect their blue books. "Is there a problem, Mr. Humphrey?" she demanded, sticking her bony chest out at him through her weirdly ugly black-and-orange striped halter dress.

Dan frowned. "Would it be all right if I ripped out the last couple pages in my blue book?" he asked, without much hope that she'd let him.

The teacher shrugged her inappropriately bare shoulders. "Go ahead."

Dan ripped the pages out before she could change her mind, surprised at her total lack of bitchiness. Maybe Ms. Solomon had finally gotten herself a boyfriend and was too busy daydreaming about the approaching hot and sexy summer of late mornings and steamy sex to bother being nasty to Dan.

Oh, like he *wasn't* daydreaming about late mornings and steamy sex? In fact, who isn't?!

who can resist an artistic page six girl?

Biology was Jenny's last exam and she'd stayed up all night studying for it. Nuclei, protozoa, osmosis—she knew it all. She answered the questions automatically, filling in the blanks without pause and making her classmates seriously jealous. Osmosis was the process in which organisms took on each other's qualities just by hanging out together. Well, if it worked for tiny little organisms, why didn't it work for them? They'd been hanging out with Jenny all year, and yet they still weren't any smarter.

And their boobs aren't much bigger, either.

I like your hair, Kim Swanson scribbled on the edge of Jessica Soames's gray plastic desktop with her number two pencil. *Can you see Jenny's answer to #21?*

Kim Swanson was the most perfectly groomed girl in the ninth grade. She'd been getting her naturally light brown hair highlighted blond since she was nine and preferred perfectly ironed Agnès B. white button-down shirts with her gray pleated uniform. It was rumored that even her underwear was ironed, and she never left the house without full makeup, a gold-and-silver Cartier chain bracelet on each wrist, and her not-so-tiny Cartier diamond studs in her ears. She spent so much time grooming herself that she hardly had time to study.

Hold on, Jessica Soames scribbled back. Jessica had been the class slut starting in fourth grade, when she'd gotten her period, and culminating in sixth grade, when she lost her virginity. She'd had the biggest chest in the class, too—until Jenny had blossomed in seventh grade, surpassing her by three whole cup sizes. Jessica stole a subtle glance at the desk to her right, trying to read the answers on Jenny's exam. But Jenny was already finished and was now doodling in calligraphy on an empty page in her blue book.

Loser, she'd written in elegant, loopy black bubble letters, and Jessica tried not to take it personally.

The truth was, Jenny had written the word to describe herself. First thing Monday morning, she'd FedExed Waverly Prep her trio of brilliant new portraits, all matted and framed, but now it was Thursday and she still hadn't heard from the admissions office. It was the first week in June. September was only three short months away, and she had nowhere to go to school. She was quietly approaching desperation.

Before they'd sat down for their exam, Elise had reminded her that Waverly was winding up the school year too and probably wouldn't get to the package she'd sent them until after their seniors graduated. But Jenny was having none of that. She'd obviously missed her chance to go to boarding school. Her only other option besides public school was to ace her exams and then beg Mrs. M to let her stay at Constance. She could repeat ninth grade, cultivate her reputation as a total geek, wear thick tortoiseshell glasses, and lengthen her uniforms to her ankles. No more appearances on Page Six. No more racy fashion spreads. No dating rock bands. No online nudity.

Aw. But isn't that what makes Jenny so special?

The problem was, she was already a straight-A student. How could she do better than she was already doing?

It occurred to Jenny that maybe her grades and her new artwork weren't enough. Why not send Waverly a copy of the

W magazine spread she'd modeled for with Serena van der Woodsen and the Page Six piece featuring a photograph of her kissing Damian, the lead guitarist from the Raves, outside the Plaza Hotel?

And while she's at it, why not send them a lock of her hair? Or one of her massive Bali support bras?

Kim Swanson snickered discreetly as she scrawled something on Jessica Soames's desk. Jenny put down her pencil and rested her forehead on her arms, her curly dark hair cascading in little ringlets all over her desk. If she sent Waverly the *W* spread and the excerpt from Page Six, she'd be the talk of the school before she even arrived. That was one way of getting people's attention, but then everyone would be so full of preconceived notions about her, she'd never change their minds. Better to earn her reputation and demand people's notice once she got there.

Ahead of her was a bizarre summer in Prague with her mother, attending some famous Czech art camp—something she'd committed to over Passover under the influence of too much Manischewitz wine. Her dad had reminded her last week, when she'd thought she'd at least have boarding school to look forward to in the fall, but now she wasn't so sure.

"Two, four, six, eight, only four more days till we graduate!" a group of seniors shrieked excitedly in the hall outside the biology lab. Then the bell rang and Jenny's classmates threw their pencils in the air and started hugging one another and signing yearbooks. Even Elise came over to ask for Kim Swanson's signature in her yearbook, and she'd despised Kim ever since Kim had spread the awful rumor that Elise had been born deformed and had had a hump in her back removed when she was two.

"Summertime," Roni Chang began to sing in her glee-club-trained falsetto, *"and the living is easy!"*

Jenny wished she could share their excitement. After all, this was her last exam. She was done for the year! Three long summer months awaited her in Europe, and the possibilities were endless. But somehow she just didn't feel like shrieking or signing anyone's yearbook, even though her calligraphy was way better than theirs.

Now she realized how the seniors must have felt all winter while they were waiting to hear back from colleges. She'd done everything she could do. Her fate was in someone else's hands.

cheating for old times' sake

Blair and Serena sat side by side at the long black chemistry lab table, scribbling away at their last and final exam. The AP chemistry students had been seated between the regular senior chemistry students and were taking a different exam, so it wasn't supposed to matter that the girls were practically bumping elbows. Constance Billard liked to think its girls were beyond cheating, but the truth was, they cheated all the time. Blair and Serena were no exception.

Molarity if 5.827 g of NaCl is diluted to a volume of 100 mL? Serena etched into the inside of her forearm with her number two pencil. She yawned and stretched, letting her arm fall on the edge of Blair's exam book.

$$n = 5.827 \text{ g} / 58.4425$$

$$n = 0.09970 \text{ mol of NaCl}$$

$$M = 0.09970 \text{ mol} / 0.100 \text{ L}$$

$$M = 0.9970 \text{ molar}$$

Blair scribbled the answer on the inside cover of her blue book. *What are you wearing Monday?* she wrote next to it.

Why Monday? Serena wrote back before copying the

answer Blair had given her. Was it possible that Blair already knew she'd been called back for a second audition?

Graduation—duh?! Blair scribbled back hastily.

Serena stared at the words Blair had written. It was so typical of her not to have realized her mistake. The second audition was on Monday—and so was graduation. Her parents were going to be there. Erik, her brother, had delayed his plans to spend the summer skiing in New Zealand with Liesl, his bodacious chick-of-the-week, so that he could be there. And Blair was giving a speech.

Oops.

You don't have to tell me if you don't want to, Blair wrote, before racing through the next two pages of her exam.

Serena watched her admiringly. Blair totally deserved to go to Yale. She was a complete whiz when it came to tests. Sunlight streamed into the chemistry lab windows and a bird chirped merrily. Serena sighed and began to scribble her name in the corner of page three of her nine-page exam.

Serena van der Woodsen. Breakfast at Fred's, *starring Serena van der Woodsen.*

Normally she didn't daydream about things like this, but this was her first chance to star in a real movie. It was hard not to want it just a little bit.

Blair folded over the last page of her exam, rapidly scribbled in the answers, and then went back to check her work. Once she was satisfied that all was correct, she glanced up at their proctor, Mrs. Crandall. The overweight, red-faced teacher was busy filing her nails, which were painted an atrocious dark beige, making her fingers look like the pig feet steeped in formaldehyde they'd had to dissect in ninth-grade bio. Blair shoved her paper out of the way and reached for Serena's.

"Hey—" Serena started to object.

"Shush," Blair whispered, already beginning to answer the unanswered questions.

Serena drew a smiley face on the page Blair was working on. It was just like old times. Except for the fact that she was with Nate, and Blair was with her new British hunk. She frowned. *And* she was going to miss graduation, which was going to make Blair hate her all over again.

Yup.

too many boys, too many choices, too little time

Vanessa kept the white Morgane Le Fay dress Blair had bought for her to wear at graduation stashed in her closet until Sunday night, the night before graduation. The lights were off in the apartment and she was all alone. She stripped down to her black-and-white striped Jockeys and slipped the dress on over her stubbly head, padding over to the full-length mirror on the back of her bedroom door to check it out.

The dress was prettier than anything she'd ever owned, with a plunging V in the satin bodice, an asymmetrical hemline, and a sort of flapper-style low waist that she'd had no idea would look as flattering on her as it did. She went back to the closet to retrieve the shoes. She and Blair had the same size feet, and Blair had left her a pair of white Michael Kors wedge-heeled sandals to go with the dress. She'd even found Vanessa a pair of cool white fishnet gloves from some consignment shop on the Upper East Side, because it was a Constance Billard tradition for the girls to wear white gloves during the ceremony.

The thing was, Vanessa wasn't going to be at the ceremony. Aaron was arriving at ten the next morning to pick her up, his red vintage Saab 900S loaded up with herbal cigarettes, soy crisps, dried edamame, and peach-flavored Snapple iced tea for their cross-country sexcapade. Her parents were in Santa Fe, New Mexico, participating in some sort of hippie artist happening, and her older sister, Ruby, was still in Finland or Poland or Lapland, developing a freaky foreign fan base for her band, SugarDaddy. It wasn't like anyone in her family cared if she missed graduation. She'd get her diploma in the mail, and Blair could return the dress. It wasn't a big deal.

Right. We believe you.

There was a scratching sound at the front door. Vanessa left her room and flicked on the living room light as someone shoved a piece of paper underneath the door. She recognized Dan's boyish scrawl before she even knelt down to pick it up.

Can't make it through graduation tomorrow without seeing you one more time. I'm upstairs.
—D

Not again!

Vanessa left the dress on and clomped upstairs to the roof in her Michael Kors wedges. It was a mild June evening, almost nine, but not quite dark. Traffic snaked on and off of the Williamsburg Bridge, and a chorus of fire alarms sounded down on Broadway. A hurricane lantern swung from the steel frame supporting the water tower. Beneath it, Dan was sitting in the lotus position, naked, with a thick paperback book open in his lap.

"What are you doing?" Vanessa demanded.

Dan looked up, his love-struck face illuminated by the lamp. He was all shimmery with it—the light and his complete adoration of her. "Wow," he murmured softly. "You look so pretty. It's almost like how—" He stopped with an embarrassed smile.

"What?" Vanessa folded her arms across her chest. If she and Dan hadn't already been best friends for so long, she might have been more upset by his freaky naked stalking appearances. But Dan was Dan—she could only muster mild irritation.

"You look like how I imagine you'd look at our wedding," Dan blurted haltingly.

Whoa.

Vanessa decided that the only appropriate response was to completely ignore what he'd said. "Is that something to do with the speech you're giving tomorrow?" She pointed at the book.

"What?" Dan looked down, like he'd forgotten it was there. "Um, sort of. Actually, not really." He closed the book and held it up, revealing all his naked manly bits. "It's called *The Sexual Art of Ecstasy*. I found it in the bookstore."

Vanessa nodded with faint interest, as if he'd just told her that it might rain later.

"There's this part about meditating together until you get to a place where you're both, like, *there*. It talks about how Sting can, like, do it forever, even though he's really old. Well, this is how he does it."

Like we really want to know.

Vanessa stared at him. Dan was sort of adorable in his own bizarre, scrawny-bodied way, but the truth was, she'd been hoping she wouldn't see him again before she left tomorrow because she didn't want to have to explain any-thing—how she loved him, but how she'd promised Aaron. How it had been sort of exciting and fun seeing two guys at once but how it had to end sometime. The truth was, she wasn't even sure how she felt, because she'd been trying not to think about it.

Dan put the book aside and held out his hand. "Or we could just kiss," he suggested with a sort of polite tenderness that made her glad he was already naked.

She went over and knelt down in front of him, careful to lift her dress up so it wouldn't touch the ground. "Just watch the dress," she warned him.

This might be her only chance to wear it. Not that she was about to tell him that.

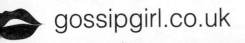
gossipgirl.co.uk

Disclaimer: All the real names of places, people, and events have been altered or abbreviated to protect the innocent. Namely, me.

hey people!

See how easy that was?

We did it! Now, if we could just decide on one of the seven dresses we bought for graduation at Bergdorf's, Barneys, *and* Bendel's because a) after popping Vivarin and bingeing on late-night pizza we didn't know if we'd gain weight or lose weight during exam week; b) we *hate* making decisions; and c) white is the new pink this summer. At least, it better be.

Boatload of european import cars unloads at ny docks last night

I'm beginning to read like the *Wall Street Journal* or something, aren't I? Anyway, if you were out and about on Park Avenue last night the way I was, you might have noticed the fleet of sleek black cars being delivered to a certain Upper East Side garage. Looks like a few of us are getting what we asked for, except . . . Dad, I asked for pink!

They know you cheated

For those of you who cheated on your final exams, we know who you are, and your teachers know, too. We saw how you finished early and spent the rest of the time writing notes and doing actressy face exercises—S!! They're only overlooking it because they want to get rid of you. Why they even bother giving seniors finals is beyond me.

A remedy for pregraduation jitters

Of course, there's nothing to be nervous about. All we have to do is look gorgeous and accept our diplomas. But we are nervous nonetheless. Maybe because we have to go through it with our parents watching. Maybe because we have no idea what comes next. You know how the school nurse always prescribes the same thing no matter what's wrong with you? Chew a Pepto-Bismol. Gargle with salt water. Well, I'm the same way: champagne and a boy. Take one dose and then repeat every fifteen minutes until symptoms subside.

Happy Graduation! See you at the party afterwards!

You know you love me.

gossip girl

pomp and circumstance

Outside Brick Church on Park Avenue and Ninety-second Street, a throng of black town cars released women in Chanel couture and men and boys in Ralph Lauren Purple Label into the church to watch their daughters and sisters graduate in Constance Billard's commencement exercises. It was a balmy June morning, and a pleasant breeze rustled the crab apple trees bordering the sidewalk, scattering petals and pretty green leaves onto the avenue. The lovely redbrick church with its sturdy white columns and creeping, well-tended green ivy looked like something out of a picture book. In fact, today the entire Upper East Side seemed picturesque and soaked in sun and apple blossom perfume, for today was graduation day.

Hooray!

Isabel's mom, Titi Coates, craned her surgically enhanced neck to survey the well-dressed audience, nearly popping the buttons on her hot-pink-and-gold Versace cap-sleeved coat-dress. "I heard Harold Waldorf flew in from Paris with his flaming French boyfriend to see Blair graduate today," she whispered to Lillian van der Woodsen, who was seated in the dark mahogany pew next to her. "He even had a red convertible Peugeot sent over in parts, with a special French mechanic to assemble it for her."

Mrs. van der Woodsen shook her head. She liked gossip, but only the harmless kind—about people's dogs or their golf game.

Harmless gossip? What would be the point?

"Harold Waldorf is in Bordeaux, at a wine auction," she corrected her tackily dressed neighbor in a polite whisper as she smoothed out the lilac-colored silk calf-length skirt of her simple-but-gorgeous Yves Saint Laurent suit. "I know for a fact because a dear friend of mine is bidding on a few bottles of Burgundy for us there. However, I know nothing about the car."

Around the corner, in one of the church's outer chambers, the seniors lined up in size order, giddily awaiting the first few chords of "Pomp and Circumstance." Kati Farkas and Isabel Coates were the shortest ones, in matching white Ferragamo flats and matching Carolina Herrera Mexican bridesmaid–style dresses with lace bows in the back and little white pom-poms hanging from the elbow-length sleeves. Desperate to be next to each other in line, they'd done a survey of all the girls in their class, asking what size heel they planned to wear for graduation. Even Doc-Marten-boots-wearing Vanessa had said she'd be wearing platforms, so flats were their best option. How cool was it that not only were they together in line, wearing matching outfits—they were *first*!

Yippee!

In her two-and-a-half-inch white kidskin Manolo dancing shoes, Blair was somewhere in the middle. Her white satin Oscar de la Renta suit had been flawlessly tailored, the jacket nipping in around her tiny waist and accentuating her excellent shoulders. None of the other girls had been creative or fashion-forward enough to even think of wearing a suit, let alone the shimmery coral pink Chanel lipstick she'd bought especially for the day or the simple pearls she'd chosen for her ears. She'd memorized her speech and kept reciting it over and over in her head, bouncing on the balls of her feet to keep her circulation going and her adrenaline level high.

Thank you for coming, ladies and gentlemen. And thank you to the senior class for electing me as its speaker. You know, some of us girls have been together since kindergarten. We learned to read together. We lost our baby teeth together. We learned how to get the most Oreos at recess together. And as the years went by, we learned not to crack under pressure together. Now here we are, college-bound, and we're all still friends. How could we not be?

There's something else I learned at Constance that I wanted to share with you today: how to get what you want. . . .

"Has anyone seen Serena?" Nicki Button asked loudly as she examined her beady brown eyes in a compact and tugged on her sweet, drop-waist, flapper-style graduation dress. "Can you believe I bought this at a *children's* vintage clothing boutique?" she asked for the tenth time so everyone could remark on how tiny and skinny she was.

"And what about Vanessa?" Laura Salmon added, sucking in her breath as she tried to tighten the semi-inappropriate lace-up bodice on her corset-style Alexander McQueen dress.

"You'd think they could try not to be late just this once," Rain Hoffstetter put in, helping Laura with her laces and trying not to bang into anyone in her inexplicably pouffy Christian Lacroix number.

Blair looked around. She'd been so preoccupied with going over her speech, she hadn't even noticed: Vanessa and Serena were missing.

Hello?

"It's nearly ten-thirty," Mrs. McLean announced urgently, clapping her meaty, freckled hands together to call the girls to order. "We'll just have to start without them."

Blair spun her ruby ring around and around on the ring finger of her left hand. Serena and Vanessa were going to *miss* graduation?! But they'd miss her speech, and anyway, *where the fuck were they??!!*

Mrs. Weeds, Constance's frizzy-haired hippie music teacher, banged out a few chords on the organ, her fat shoulder blades jiggling in a strapless Laura Ashley number. "All right, girls, this is it!" Mrs. McLean shouted excitedly. "Your last hurrah as Constance girls." She raised her freckled fist in the air, her red, white, and blue Talbots special-occasion suit wrinkling with the strain. "Make it a good one!" she added, looking dykier than ever.

"Ooh!" the audience gasped as the girls began to march into the main hall of the church and down the lily-strewn center aisle in time to the music, looking like crosses between runway models and mail-order brides.

Eleanor Waldorf Rose sat between her husband of less than one year, Cyrus Rose, and Blair's twelve-year-old brother, Tyler. Eleanor was the only woman in the room wearing a wide-brimmed dove gray Philip Treacy hat with actual dove feathers in it.

Exactly where did she think she was—England?

Cyrus Rose was wearing a remarkably ugly avocado-colored double-breasted Hugo Boss suit and was jiggling Yale, Blair's six-week-old baby sister, on his knee. Yale had on the Burberry kilt Blair had bought for her even before she was born and a white eyelet onesie that Blair had ordered from Oeuf, a baby boutique in Paris. Tyler looked hungover. Or maybe Blair just hadn't seen him in so long, she'd forgotten what he looked like even though he was her brother. And Aaron appeared to be missing.

Wonder why.

When Blair reached their pew, Eleanor leapt to her feet and blew her a kiss, snapping away with her baby pink Nokia camera-phone while tears oozed down her overly rouged cheeks. "We're so proud of you," she gushed in a voice that was definitely louder than a whisper.

Farther down the aisle Mrs. van der Woodsen caught Blair's eye and beamed at her proudly, as if Blair were her own daughter. Blair shrugged her shoulders apologetically, although she was pretty sure Serena's mom hadn't quite realized that Serena was missing. Poor Mr. and Mrs. van der Woodsen. Even Erik, Serena's hot junior-at-Brown brother whom Blair had almost lost her virginity to over spring break, was there.

Blair had never met Vanessa's parents, but Vanessa had described them to her pretty well, and she didn't see any gray-haired, inappropriately dressed hippies in the audience. She decided to keep her eyes on the chestnut brown ponytail of the girl in front of her in line, who happened to be Rain Hoffstetter, whom she happened to kind of hate. All Blair had to do was make her speech, which she'd memorized so thoroughly, she could recite it in her sleep, and then get her diploma. Then she was going to have the best graduation party anyone had ever been to, have sex with Marcus, take a carriage ride in Central Park, and then he'd ask her to marry him. . . . Her eyes misted over dreamily and she stepped on the back of Rain's puffy white dress, nearly knocking her over.

Focus, focus!

One by one the girls filed in and seated themselves in the first three rows of pews. Thirty-four seniors in total, not counting the missing two. Mrs. McLean stood at the pulpit, waiting to address the outgoing class and their families. Blair would give her speech directly afterwards, and then the guest speaker, "Auntie Lynn," some old lady who'd basically founded the Girl Scouts or something, was supposed to talk. Auntie Lynn was already leaning on her metal walker in the front row, wearing a poo-brown pantsuit and hearing aids in both ears, looking sleepy and bored. After she spoke—or keeled over and died, whichever came first—Mrs. McLean would hand out the diplomas.

Mrs. Weeds crashed through the last few chords of "Pomp and Circumstance." "Let us pray," Mrs. McLean directed somberly and bowed her head. The headmistress had become deeply religious after her husband, Randall, had died in a deep-sea fishing accident in the Florida Keys. At least, that was the story the girls told, along with the one about Mrs. McLean's girlfriend, Vonda, who lived in Mrs. McLean's country house up in Woodstock, New York, and drove a tractor. Mrs. McLean had the words *Ride me, Vonda* tattooed on her inner thigh. There was even a rumor that Vonda used to *be* Randall, but none of the girls knew for sure.

"I heard Serena and Nate eloped to Mustique. That's why she's not here," Rain whispered to Laura. "She's wearing her graduation dress as a wedding dress. Remember how we saw her trying on that veil in Vera Wang?" she added knowingly.

"And I heard Vanessa is pregnant," Laura replied. "She's up in Vermont with her parents, dealing. I guess she'll probably still get her diploma anyway."

Blair tried unsuccessfully not to listen, but of course she was dying to know where Serena and Vanessa were herself. Had Vanessa gone off somewhere with Aaron? Or Dan? Had Serena and Nate *really* eloped? It was such a crazy day and such a crazy time in their lives, she wasn't sure what to believe.

"And now, I'm delighted to introduce Blair Waldorf, our senior class speaker," Mrs. McLean announced. With a bob of her Raggedy Ann auburn head, she stepped away from the podium to make way for Blair. Blair stood up, smoothed out her swishy, pleated white satin Oscar de la Renta skirt, and climbed daintily over the pointy white-shoe-clad feet of her classmates, growing steadily more and more enraged as she overheard snatches of their whispers and mutterings.

"Serena is so totally not going to Yale next year."

"Vanessa is in L.A. Didn't you hear? She's making a movie with Brad Pitt."

Blair mounted the steps to the podium—a vision of perfection with her Oscar-tailored satin suit, her smooth and shiny dark bob, her long-lashed bright blue eyes, her glittering coral-colored mouth, and her exquisite white shoes. She cleared her throat, trying to tear everyone's attention away from the subject of the two missing girls.

"Thank you," she began. "First, I'd like to congratulate my class. We made it!" she cried with exaggerated glee. But none of her fucking classmates were even looking at her.

Who cares? Who cares? Who cares? She was graduating today, she had an amazing new boyfriend who just happened to be an English lord, and in the fall she was off to Yale. That was all that mattered, she told herself as she continued her speech. And that she looked seriously hot in her sleek Oscar de la Renta suit while all the other girls looked like Little Bo Beep in their frilly white dresses.

"Now here we are, college-bound, and we're all still friends," Blair declared determinedly.

Sure they are.

oh, the places you'll go!—not

Daaah, dee-dee-dee, daaah, daaah . . .

St. Jude's didn't bother renting out a church or lining their boys up in size order. They just held a small, solemn ceremony in the school's rooftop gym, wished the boys well, and then sent them on their way. The usually cavernous-looking gym seemed smaller now, filled as it was with folding chairs, mothers in Chanel jackets and over-the-knee linen skirts, and dads in Brooks Brothers summer-weight gray flannel suits.

Nate had been waiting for this day forever, and to mark the occasion, he and his buddies had gotten good and high at Charlie's house beforehand. Then they'd put on their burgundy-colored school ties and their navy blue wool school jackets with the dorky brass buttons that they'd never, ever have to wear again, and walked over.

He glanced over his shoulder at his parents, seated stiffly across the aisle and six rows back. Captain Archibald met his gaze and waved the graduation program angrily in front of him, stabbing at the list of graduates with his index finger, his gray-blond eyebrows knitted together in outrage.

Nate picked up the program where it had fallen between his Church's of London tan suede lace-ups and studied it to see if he could figure out what his dad's problem was. Forty-three boys' names were printed neatly in navy blue in two concise columns. The very first name on the list had a tiny asterisk next to it, and at the very bottom of the program, next to a matching tiny asterisk, was the note, *Diploma pending*. Nate squinted, wondering if his thoroughly baked brain was playing tricks on him, but there it was again, an asterisk next to his name—*Nathaniel Fitzwilliam Archibald.* * *Diploma pending*.

Fuck!

Father Mark, the ancient former pastor who'd been the St. Jude's principal since at least 1947, hunkered over the podium set up in the front of the gym, his hands shaking as he began to read out the boys' names. Of course Nate was first. "Nathaniel Fitzwilliam Archibald!"

Nate stood up and walked to the front of the gym, keeping his eyes on the black and blue lines duct-taped to the floor for hoops and floor hockey. "Way to go, man," a bunch of guys whispered sarcastically. Nate's neck burned with shame. There was an asterisk next to his name.

Father Mark handed him a square navy blue faux leather folder and shook his hand just like he was supposed to, without any acknowledgment of the asterisk. Nate turned around and walked back to his seat, nearly colliding with Coach Michaels, who was blocking the aisle in his frigging red Lands' End windbreaker. He grabbed Nate's shirtsleeve and lunged forward to whisper in his ear. "I've got your number, boy," he wheezed, then patted Nate roughly on the shoulder before letting him go.

"Aw. Isn't that sweet?" somebody's mother cooed, mistaking Coach's threat for a congratulatory embrace.

Nate returned to his seat, breathless and sweaty. "Anthony Arthur Avuldsen!" the old principal croaked, impatiently waving the blue folder containing Anthony's diploma over his white-peach-fuzz-covered head.

Anthony lumbered over Nate's khaki-pants-clad knees with stoned concentration. Nate clapped his friend on his muscular back. "You made it," he murmured weakly as the now-familiar choky, about-to-cry feeling welled up in his throat.

"Charles Cameron Dern!" Father Mark croaked hoarsely.

"Dude," Charlie murmured to Nate as he stumbled by, "what's with the little star?"

Nate was too perplexed to cry. He just sat there in stoned numbness, his father's furious stare burning holes in his back as his fellow classmates collected their diplomas. The blue leather folder lay closed on his lap. He nudged it open with his thumb just a crack. Just as he'd suspected: The folder was empty.

Oh, boy.

Directly behind old Father Mark was the black metal door with the words PHYSICAL EDUCATION DEPARTMENT stenciled on it in white. Nate stared at the door, his glittering green eyes blinking in consternation. Did the asterisk have something to do with Coach's Viagra?

Finally, he's catching on!

d could use a little more love

"So in conclusion, who needs college—at least, right now? I've got my whole life to get educated. Just like John Lennon of the Beatles once wrote, 'Love is all you need. Love is all you need. Love is all you need.'"

Dan surveyed the audience as he finished his speech, standing behind the wooden podium at the front of the stage. Riverside Prep's informal graduation ceremony was held in the school auditorium and felt very much like one of the off-kilter plays the drama department put on twice a year. Behind him, Dan's forty-one other classmates were seated on folding chairs, their mouths hanging open in shocked surprise. Even Larry, their desperate-to-be-down-with-the-boys senior homeroom teacher, kept chuckling nervously and glancing down at the thirty rows of faculty, parents, and relatives seated in the gray velvet movie-theater-style seats below them, as if he were wondering if he should explain that Dan's speech was just another one of those goofy senior pranks he and his boyz were always pullin'.

In the last row of seats, Rufus's head was bowed, his fuzzy salt-and-pepper hair tied with the festive orange ribbon that had come tied around the neck of the bottle of Veuve Clicquot champagne he'd bought for them to drink later. Jenny was holding his hand. She looked up, meeting Dan's gaze across the rows of heads with her soulful brown eyes. *You asshole, how could you do this to our sweet, well-meaning dad?* her expression seemed to say. *In case you didn't remember, education is everything to him.*

Dan remained onstage to receive the E. B. White Writing Award, Riverside Prep's award for outstanding creative writing achievement. "Congratulations, son." Their lisping, tall, young, Russian-figure-skater-handsome principal, Dr. Nesbitt, handed him the rolled-up piece of parchment paper and shook his hand while a photographer snapped pictures. Dr. Nesbitt was a lower-school dad who'd been acting principal for a year and a half—ever since Mr. Coobie, the previous principal, had gotten ousted after attempting to teach human development to the fifth graders himself instead of hiring a professional.

The applause was thin and sporadic as Dan accepted the award and returned to his seat. It was bound to be after a speech like that. *Don't listen to your teachers? Let love be your teacher and follow your heart? Love is all you need, love is all you need, love is all you need?*

Hello??!

"And now for the diplomas," Dr. Nesbitt announced, and the audience shifted eagerly in their seats.

None of the boys' last names began with *A*, so Chuck Bass was first. For the occasion, Chuck had dressed entirely in cream-colored linen, including his shoes, which were made by Hogan and even had cream-colored crepe soles. With his sleek, dark hair and tanned handsome face, he actually looked pretty sharp, like a Hollywood star from the 1940s. Chuck tucked the brown-leather-bound diploma case under his arm, pulled a Cuban cigar out of his jacket pocket, and put it between his lips.

He was about to turn and walk offstage when Dr. Nesbitt snatched the cigar out of his mouth, wiped it on his trousers, and stuck it in his own mouth. "I'm going to need something to chew on to get through all these names," he quipped into the microphone, and the audience of parents responded with a roar of laughter. Dr. Nesbitt had been so popular since stepping in as principal, he'd had to temporarily shut down his psychiatric practice because the school had yet to find a new principal they liked nearly as much.

"Nice speech, dickhead," Chuck hissed as he lumbered over Dan's feet on his way back to his seat. "'Follow your heart'? Does that mean we're eloping to Vegas together after the ceremony?" Dan resisted the urge to grind his Wallabees into Chuck's nuts. He hadn't thought about how his speech might sound to everyone else. All he knew was that he'd written it from the heart, with one person in mind: Vanessa.

"Nice work," Zeke Freedman sneered at Dan as he passed by on his way up to the stage. Zeke and Dan had been best buddies until Vanessa became Dan's girlfriend and Dan sort of forgot about everything and everybody else. Zeke was kind of a computer geek and was extremely proud of the fact that he was going to MIT in the fall, so it wasn't a stretch to guess that Dan's speech had rubbed him the wrong way.

Dan glanced back at his family again. Jenny had her arm around their dad now, and Rufus's shoulders were shaking with grief. The other parents probably thought Rufus was weeping with pride, but Dan knew better. Maybe he should have given his dad some warning and told him about not going to Evergreen next year.

Yeah, maybe.

"Daniel Jonah Humphrey," Dr. Nesbitt called out.

Dan squirmed in his seat. Hadn't he used up enough front-of-stage time already? He dashed out of his third-row seat, grabbed the brown leather folder out of Dr. Nesbitt's hand, and dashed back to his seat again, as if he were afraid his classmates were going to pelt him with raw tomatoes or something.

Jenny had thought Dan's graduation would be relatively

painless and boring. She hadn't even minded when her dad had changed her ticket to Prague to leave tomorrow morning instead of yesterday so she wouldn't miss it. He'd get his diploma while she and Rufus whispered to each other and heckled his nerdy classmates. Then they'd go eat Chinese at Dan's favorite place on Broadway, and later she'd drag Dan out to that party Blair Waldorf was rumored to be hosting at the Yale Club—a party that she was absolutely determined not to miss.

Instead, their whole family was falling apart, and she was freaking out.

She and Dan had basically stopped being nice to each other when Jenny had spent the night in a Plaza Hotel room with the members of the Raves and then proceeded to record a song with them on the same day they fired Dan. At home it seemed like Dan could do no wrong. He was a published author and an A student. He'd had his pick of colleges to go to, including Brown, Colby, NYU, and Evergreen. Their dad boasted about his achievements all the time. Jenny was an even better student, but ever since Mrs. McLean had requested that she not return to Constance next year, she'd felt like Dan's naughty little sister. The fact that overprotective Rufus had actually agreed to let her go to boarding school made it even more clear: Dan was the good one, and she was the bad one.

But now here she was, holding her dad's hand and pretending to be totally calm and mentally stable while she was really wondering what was going to become of *her* next year. If only she could take Dan's place at Evergreen. It was supposed to be arty—she'd probably do fine.

Too bad they don't have a tenth grade.

a reads v like a book

Even though she'd been totally two-timing him and a cross-country road trip really wasn't her idea of a good time, Vanessa was ready for Aaron when he pulled up in his red Saab, right on time. She just couldn't let him down, because if she did, she'd have to explain her outrageously heinous behavior, which she wasn't prepared to do, because she honestly didn't know why she'd behaved so heinously. Maybe she was just . . .

Psycho?

"I'll be down in a sec!" she called when he buzzed from downstairs.

"Nah, buzz me in, I'm coming up," he responded.

Vanessa should have known that something was up when he walked in and didn't kiss her. Downstairs, Mookie, Aaron's huge brown-and-white boxer, barked eagerly out of the Saab's open sunroof.

There were green beads in Aaron's coarse brown hair. All of a sudden Vanessa noticed that he'd grown it out into inch-long little dreads all over his head. When had that happened?

"Thank God Blair's graduating today too," he remarked. "My dad was totally fine with going to her thing instead of mine." He patted his green army-issue-shorts pockets. "Um . . ." he began, his dark eyes darting nervously around the room. "Hey, nice dress!"

The Morgane le Fay dress hung all by itself in the living room closet.

Vanessa shrugged. "I'm returning it."

Aaron went over to the dress and pulled the hanger off the rail, twirling it around to get the full effect of the dress. "Put it on," he suggested, holding it out to her.

She shook her head. "I already tried it on a couple of times. Besides graduation, I don't have anywhere else to wear it."

Aaron hung on to the dress. "Look," he began. "I kind of don't think it's a good idea for you to come with me. First of all, with Mookie I kind of don't have any more room in my car. Second of all, I've kind of known for a while that you and Dan have kind of been hanging out a lot."

Kind of.

Vanessa crossed her arms over her chest, all of a sudden feeling a little too large or a little too stupid or a little too something she couldn't quite place. He *knew*? But hadn't she and Dan been totally discreet?

You call having sex in broad daylight on a rooftop discreet?!

"I'm sorry," she managed to utter. It was all she could think of.

"It's okay. But you should have told me when I tried to give you this." Aaron held out the corny silver joined-hearts love/friendship ring. "I found it in a drawer with the serving spoons." He didn't even look that upset, which made Vanessa feel even worse. Obviously she'd been paying so little attention that he'd had time to think about this and get over it. But aside from feeling terrible, she was also totally relieved.

Aaron held up the dress again and twirled it around on its hanger. "I also kind of think you don't want to miss graduation. You love those girls," he added gently, sounding only slightly gay.

"Yeah, right," Vanessa agreed sarcastically, but again she felt totally relieved. She could wear the dress even though she was supposed to hate white. She could sit next to Blair and make fun of Mrs. M and finally graduate, and the whole class would get drunk together afterwards, even though they were all supposed to hate each other.

Okay, maybe she did love those girls just a little bit.

Aaron waggled the dress in front of her. "You know you want to."

Vanessa snorted and snatched it out of his hands, catching him in a hug as she did so. "Don't think you're getting away without kissing me good-bye. I don't know when I'm ever going to see you again."

She kissed him quickly on the lips and then pressed her forehead into his warm, familiar shoulder, her body a bundle of nerves. She was breaking up with her boyfriend, she was about to graduate, there was a party to go to, and a whole four years at NYU awaited her, with no more stupid fucking uniforms!

Yippee! Except, hasn't she sort of forgotten about someone?

Vanessa changed into her dress right in front of Aaron, feeling almost sisterly toward him now that they were broken up. She still loved him and probably always would. But the great thing about love was that it *evolved*.

Let's make sure she remembers that.

"What do you think?" she asked, doing a Barbie-esque spin in Blair's white wedge-heeled shoes.

Aaron flinched, as if it hurt to see her looking so incredibly gorgeous. He held out his hand. "Come on. I heard on the radio the subways are a mess. I'll drive you."

Aw. How come boys get so much cuter after we break up with them?

who's that girl?

"And that is why I'm standing here today in a pair of limited-edition Manolo Blahnik dancing shoes and an Oscar de la Renta suit that was tailored just for me," Blair told her audience with an indulgent smile as she wound up her speech. "Don't ever let anyone tell you you should be happy with what you have. There's always more, and there's no reason you shouldn't have it all."

Everyone in the church remained politely silent, as if they weren't quite sure whether she'd finished her speech or not.

Not that anyone was actually paying attention.

"Hey, is that who I think it is?" Kati Farkas whispered to Isabel Coates. The two girls craned their necks to see over their classmates' heads as Vanessa appeared in one of the church's side entrances. Her face was a happy pink and her dress a stunning white. Her wedge-heeled shoes were awesome, and her little white fishnet gloves were outstanding. She looked so different from her normally black-clad, frowning self, she was barely recognizable.

"Yeah, and she actually looks kind of . . . *good*," Isabel remarked reluctantly. "Of course, Blair picked out her dress. Otherwise she probably would've come wrapped in a white sheet or something."

Actually, Vanessa *had* flirted with the sheet idea, but the Morgane Le Fay dress was so much more flattering.

"Um, that's all," Blair announced from her place at the podium. She looked around for Mrs. M, and that's when she noticed Vanessa. First Blair narrowed her eyes to show that she was pissed as hell at Vanessa for being so late. Then she gave her friend and former roommate a thumbs-up for looking so completely amazing. The audience broke out into weak applause as she made her way back to her seat.

"Thank you, Blair." Mrs. M said, taking her place at the podium. "And now, the moment you've all been waiting for. It is my pleasure to hand out the diplomas to the graduating class. Vanessa Marigold Abrams, don't bother finding a seat. You're first." She flashed Vanessa one of her rare and famous warm smiles, forgiving her most alternative graduating senior for missing half the ceremony.

Marigold?! That's what you get when you have hippie artist parents.

Vanessa strutted to the front of the room in her awesome shoes, ears burning at the sound of her ridiculous middle name and eyes shiny with tears, full of love for everyone there, including Mrs. M. She couldn't believe she'd almost missed this. Clasping the burgundy-leather-bound diploma case in her hand, her big brown eyes shiny with happy tears, she hugged the headmistress like she was her long-lost grandma.

"I'm also extremely proud to bestow on you, Vanessa Marigold, the Georgia O'Keeffe Award for creative excellence," Mrs. M announced. She placed a light blue satin ribbon around Vanessa's neck. From it hung a gold-plated medal embossed with one of Georgia O'Keeffe's vaginalike poppies. "Congratulations."

Vanessa hopped offstage and walked down the center aisle of the church to Blair's third-row pew. "Can I sit here?"

"Move over," Blair told Rain. Rain was wearing a white

tulle dress that looked like an oversized tutu from *Swan Lake*. "Your dress doesn't need *that* much room."

"Isabel Siobhan Coates," Mrs. M called, holding up Isabel's diploma.

Vanessa wedged herself in beside Blair and grabbed the graduation program out of her hands. "Shit. Sorry I missed your speech."

No she's not.

"That's okay." Blair tugged on Vanessa's dress. "Tell me you don't love this and I'll totally kill you. You should wear white, like, every day."

Vanessa blotted her tears with her thumbs and flipped open the burgundy leather case holding her diploma. "Check it out," she breathed. Both girls studied the gold-embossed piece of parchment paper upon which was printed Vanessa's name, followed by the date and the name of their school, and then a whole bunch of stuff in Latin. It was totally official looking and totally worthless looking at the same time. All those years of uniforms and too much homework for *this*?

Vanessa flipped the case closed and held it tight to her chest. She didn't care—she'd made it! And her whole future lay ahead of her. After taking every film course NYU offered, she'd become a famous indie filmmaker, except she'd stick to true indies—unlike her former mentor, Ken Mogul, who was totally selling out with that teen movie he was making at Barneys. It was a good thing Aaron had broken up with her today, because now she was free to meet all sorts of interesting people from around the globe, and she could experiment with different relationships. After all, wasn't that what college was all about?

Yeah, maybe. But again, isn't she kind of forgetting about someone??

some would argue that her last name begins with **w**

"Serena Caroline van der Woodsen," Mrs. M called out.

"Shit," Blair muttered under her breath. Where the fuck *was* Serena, anyway? She glanced back at the other van der Woodsens. They looked perky and excited. Unbelievably, they still hadn't quite grasped the fact that Serena was missing.

"Serena? Are you present?" asked the headmistress, scanning the church with her glassy brown eyes. "Has anyone seen Serena?" The pretty, never-quite-reaching-her-potential blonde was forever late for morning assemblies, but one would have thought she could pull it together to be on time for this particular event.

The other girls twittered. No one offered the headmistress an answer. Blair glanced back at Serena's family once more. Now they looked confused, although the van der Woodsens never lost their cool. Erik jutted his chin at Blair, silently suggesting that she go up to accept Serena's diploma for her.

"Blair Cornelia Waldorf," Mrs. M announced sternly. No Constance girl had ever missed graduation before, and she was cross now, very cross. She'd allowed Serena to come back to Constance after she'd been thrown out of boarding school, and now Serena couldn't even be bothered to turn up for commencement?

Thank goodness Blair's *W* came right after Serena's *V*. In fact, some would argue Serena's last name began with *W* and therefore came after Blair's. Not that it mattered or that anyone really cared at this point.

Blair went up to the podium to receive her diploma. "I'll take Serena's for her," she whispered, hoping her voice wouldn't carry over the microphone.

Mrs. M smiled tersely and shook her hand. "That won't be necessary," she replied, nodding at something over Blair's shoulder.

Blair spun around to find Serena sprinting up the aisle in *her* suit—exactly the same white satin Oscar de la Renta suit with the swishy pleated knee-length skirt that she herself was wearing. And because Serena was practically a foot taller than Blair and they both weighed the same, it looked even better on Serena, despite the fact that she was barefoot, her hair was all over the place, and she'd forgotten her gloves.

"Sorry, Mrs. M!" Serena panted, flashing their headmistress the famously charming smile that had won over everyone from avant-garde artists to the admissions offices at Yale, Brown, Harvard, and everywhere else she'd applied. "Just think—this is the last time I'll ever be late!"

Blair wanted to slap her for being so charming when she should have been in serious trouble. In fact, Serena probably would've failed chemistry and not graduated if it hadn't been for her. She hated the way they must look standing side by side in their matching suits. People probably thought they'd bought them together or something. One thing was for sure— Blair was definitely making Serena change her outfit before her big party at the Yale Club tonight. No fucking way was she allowing Marcus to see how much better Serena looked in that damned suit.

Mrs. M had had enough. Half an hour of shaking parents' hands and offering a few lame anecdotes about their sweet, intelligent daughters, and she was off to Woodstock for the summer to watch Vonda weed their heirloom tomato collection wearing only the red embroidered halter top Mrs. M had bought for her at a craft fair last weekend.

"Take your seats, girls," she ordered, dismissing Blair and Serena.

They walked back to the pews. There was no room for Serena, so she perched on Vanessa's knee.

"You have my blessings." Mrs. M blew the seniors a kiss. "And now, class is dismissed!"

Whoooopppeeee!

her heart is on some other boy's sleeve

After the ceremony, Nate did a few bong hits with the other boys in the billiard room over at Jeremy's, but his heart wasn't in it. They were all high school graduates, while he was still "diploma pending." Whatever the fuck that meant.

Leaving them to celebrate without him, he meandered slowly west on Eighty-sixth Street toward home, thankful that his parents had been so pissed off at him for that goddamned asterisk that they'd gone straight up to Mt. Desert Island for the week, leaving him in peace. Up in his room, he began to sort through his cedar walk-in closet. On the shelf above the clothes rail, behind that ridiculous Darth Vader head he'd worn for Halloween two years in a row back in fourth and fifth grade, was the little mahogany pirate's treasure chest with the brass lock that his uncle Gerard had given him when he was eight, where Nate stowed all his old photographs. He grabbed the clothes rail with one hand and used it to steady himself as he scaled the closet wall with his bare feet, trying to get the fucker down.

The chest spilled open on the floor. There he was on a fishing boat in Prince William Sound up in Alaska two Augusts ago with his arm around his dad, both smiling like losers and wearing dirty yellow foul-weather gear. That was the best time he and his dad had ever had together. Fishing in

the weird eleven o'clock twilight, surrounded by ghostly gla-
ciers, and sharing a flask of Scotch on their way back into
port. Then there were the pictures of him and Blair. He looking bored and sleepy and embarrassed, with his head on her
rose-colored pillows, and she looking crazily ecstatic, with her
cheek pressed violently into his ear as she held her camera in
front of their faces and snapped the pictures herself.

Then there was the picture of Serena's elegant, tanned
foot with the words *Miss you* written on it in purple marker
that she'd sent him last year while she was still up at boarding
school. Nate had kept it, loving her sexy silver toe ring, and
loving how he knew it was from her, even though she hadn't
sent it with a note or used a return address or anything. He
held the photograph in his hands, trying to invoke that tingly,
turned-on feeling he'd felt when he'd gotten it in the mail,
but now it was just a silly old photograph that didn't really
invoke anything.

He glanced at the photo of him and Blair again, missing
the way they used to kick around together doing stupid
things, like drinking way too many vodka tonics before a
movie and then running out during the previews because
they couldn't stop laughing. Her new-shoe-and-Kiehl's-
cucumber-skin-cream smell. The way she was so sexy when
she was throwing a fit. He wanted her to sit on his lap. He
wanted her hands in his pockets. He wanted her to call him at
seven o'clock in the morning on a Sunday because she was
hyper and couldn't wait for him to wake up.

He tossed the photos back in the pirate's chest and closed
the lid. Hanging on the clothes rail inside a clear plastic bag
was the moss green cashmere sweater Blair had given him last
spring. The maid had sent it to the dry cleaners so it would
be ready for Nate to wear at Yale in the fall. Nate ripped open
the bag and felt inside the sweater's right sleeve. No, maybe it
was the left. Yes, there it was. The tiny gold heart pendant
Blair had sewn inside it so that he would always be wearing

her heart on his sleeve. Blair probably thought he hadn't noticed the heart, but he wore the sweater so much, how could he not have? He loved that sweater.

Sounds like the love went beyond knitwear.

Tears began to seep out of the corners of Nate's green eyes as he grasped the gold heart pendant between his thumb and forefinger and ripped it out of the sweater's sleeve. His phone rang before he could decide what to do next.

Hopefully nothing too rash.

"Hello?"

"It's been a rocky year for you, son," Coach Michaels barked on the other end of the line. "I thought you were over all that drug nonsense. Then you have to go and steal my damned Viagra? What's wrong with you, boy?"

"I'm sorry," Nate mumbled almost inaudibly. He was already crying. Coach couldn't make him feel much worse.

"I had a long talk with Dr. Nesbitt and your dad after the ceremony," Coach continued, "and you're one lucky kid."

Lucky? It wasn't exactly the first word that came to Nate's mind.

"Withholding your diploma was just a little slap on the wrist to let you know you can't get away with stealing my stuff, especially my medication. Your real punishment comes this summer. I've got a place out in the Hamptons that could use some fixing up. So if you want to play lacrosse for Yale next year, you gotta be my boy this summer. Live over the garage, work for me, and in your spare time, you'll be going to the local church for AA meetings."

Nate swallowed hard. He'd imagined a lazy summer up in Maine getting tan and helping his dad with the boats, but he had no choice. He had to be the coach's Hamptons bitch for the summer. "Sorry for being such a dick, Coach," he said earnestly. "I promise to make it up to you."

Coach Michaels chuckled. "Then at least you'll be a dick with a diploma!"

Nate forced himself to chuckle along with the old man. Things were going to be okay, he told himself. He'd have his diploma by the end of the summer.

"Thanks, Coach." He hung up and opened his damp hand to look at the gold heart pendant.

Well, *some* things were going to be okay.

He sighed the sort of shuddering, exhausted sigh that comes after a long cry and tossed the heart onto his neatly made bed. Then he went back to rummaging through his closet. He was supposed to meet Serena at Blair's Yale Club party at seven o'clock. Maybe she'd come up with a way to make *everything* okay.

Without any Viagra.

will j resort to homeschooling?

"I guess I failed to raise you properly." Rufus sighed heavily as he stared into a troughlike glass of red wine. The way he saw it, you had two choices in this city. Either you spent an arm and a leg to send your kids to private school, where they learned to shop for insanely expensive clothes and to be snobbish to their father, but also to converse in Latin, memorize Keats, and do algorithms in their heads; or, you sent them to public school, where they might not learn to read, might not graduate, and risked getting shot. He'd thought he'd done the right thing. But now it looked like neither of his kids was going to any school of any kind next year.

"You didn't fail, Dad," Dan corrected as he scarfed down a forkful of sesame noodles. Rufus and Jenny had waited outside Hunan 92 on Ninety-second and Amsterdam while he went in to buy some celebratory takeout. He'd stayed up all night working on his speech, drinking instant coffee after instant coffee and smoking Camel after Camel. If he didn't eat something, he wasn't going to make it to any party later. Now they were home, sitting at the dining room table, staring at one another, with an unopened bottle of champagne on the table. It was a Monday and barely four o'clock—an odd time to all be home together.

"At least he got into college," Jenny put in glumly. She'd

worn a new stretchy lavender-and-pale-yellow Pucci print wrap dress to Dan's graduation, and there were two huge damp spots under each pendulous boob from where she'd sweated in the heat. She felt disgusting and was particularly resentful of her brother and father for being in such equally bad moods that they weren't even going to try to cheer her up. She thought about calling Elise, but she was at her country house in Cape Cod, and she'd only make Jenny feel worse by moping about the fact that they were going to be apart next year. That is, if Jenny was actually going anywhere next year. As things stood, she might have to be homeschooled.

She glanced at her father. In an effort to fit in with the other fathers, he'd worn a suit to Dan's graduation, but it was black wool—too warm for June, and all wrong with the weirdly trendy, tight-fitting pumpkin orange shirt he'd borrowed from Dan to wear underneath it. He'd yanked out the orange ribbon in his fury, and his wiry salt-and-pepper hair was now fashioned into a sort of messy chignon, held together with the electric blue magnetic bulldog clip they used to keep their takeout menus on the door of the refrigerator. To make things worse, there were stray pieces of pink towel lint in his beard.

Maybe homeschooling wasn't such a great idea.

"Isn't there someplace you kids need to be?" Rufus asked, downing the remains of his wine. Obviously, one glass wouldn't be nearly enough.

"Come on, Dad," Dan complained. "It's not like I'm never going to college. I just deferred for a year, that's all."

Rufus reached for the uncorked bottle of Sangiovese in the middle of the table and poured himself some more. "I just spent eighty thousand dollars on your high school education, all borrowed, so it'll probably be double with interest. Excuse me for not being ecstatic." His gray eyebrows knitted together in a furry single line. "Does Vanessa even know about this?" he demanded suspiciously.

Dan ripped open a clear plastic packet of fluorescent orange duck sauce with his teeth and squirted it onto an egg roll. "Not really."

Jenny and Rufus both stared at him in shocked surprise.

Dan looked up. "What?"

"Idiot," Jenny breathed across the table at him. She'd worked with Vanessa Abrams on *Rancor*, the Constance student-run arts magazine, and had hung out with her enough times to know that she was fiercely independent and not at all into this sort of lovesick-puppy-dog shit Dan was pulling. Besides, wasn't she supposed to be going out with Blair Waldorf's stepbrother now? "Idiot," she muttered again.

Rufus didn't say anything. He just picked up his glass of wine, carried it out of the dining room, down the hall, and into his office, slamming the door shut behind him.

Dan shrugged his shoulders and opened up another packet of duck sauce. "I really don't know what everyone's problem is."

Jenny was about to tell him what an ignorant, presumptuous asshole he was when her baby blue Nokia began to jingle with the first few notes of "Happy Birthday to You," the Raves recording she'd sung backup for. She bit her lip, still glaring at Dan with her big brown eyes.

"It's your phone. You better answer it," Dan told her with his mouth full.

"Fine." Jenny reached into her imitation–Louis Vuitton Calla Lily purse and pressed the yes button on her phone. It was probably Elise, calling her from Cape Cod to complain about how bored she was of eating lobster with her parents. "Just to warn you, I'm in a really bad mood," Jenny said in greeting.

There was silence on the other end.

"Hello?" Jenny demanded impatiently.

"Yes? Is this Jennifer Humphrey?" a polite male voice replied.

Oops.

She sat up straight in her chair. "Speaking."

Jenny reminded Dan of someone just then, but he couldn't quite place who. Their mother, maybe? Except the only real memory he had of his mother was of her trying to teach him how to tie a tie when he was only five. He'd kept messing up because her perfume was so pungent, it had made him dizzy.

"This is Thaddeus Moore, director of admissions at Waverly Prep," the man introduced himself. "Do you have a moment?"

Did she ever!

"Yes," she answered cautiously, her heart beating so hard, she could practically feel her ribs cracking. Dan's pack of Camel filters was sitting on the table. She reached for them and pulled one out, tapping it on the tabletop like a veteran smoker. If only her dad had left the wine behind.

"Good. Well, I wanted to let you know that we received your application and the package you sent, and we were very impressed, especially with your artwork," Mr. Moore informed her. "I myself spoke with your headmistress, Mrs. McLean, and she couldn't say enough kind, enthusiastic things about you. Of course, applications for next fall have been closed since December. However, due to unexpected circumstances, a space has just opened up for the fall. So if you're still interested in attending Waverly next year, we'd be happy to have you."

Jenny whipped the unlit cigarette at her brother and it bounced off his stupid, staring forehead and onto the floor. "Really?!" she nearly shouted. "Oh my God. Really?!"

"Yes, really," Mr. Moore responded with what sounded like a tinge of amusement. "We'll send you the paperwork today if you like."

Oh, what a nice, *nice* man. "Yes, please!" Jenny stood up and then sat down again. She was so excited, she thought she might wet her wrap dress. "Thank you. Oh my God. Thank you so much!"

"You're quite welcome."

She realized she should hang up before she said something really stupid and he changed his mind. "I better go tell my father now. I'm so glad you called. Thank you."

Jenny hung up, danced around the table, and threw her arms around Dan. "I'm going to boarding school!" she shrieked giddily, grabbing his shoulders and shaking his skinny, smelly body like a rag doll. "I'm going to boarding school!"

"Cool," Dan responded, relieved that the attention had shifted away from his own dubious predicament. He fished a fortune cookie out of the bottom of the paper bag he'd brought his Chinese food home in. "Good for you."

Jenny spun around and hurtled toward her dad's office. Ignoring the strict rule Rufus had laid down when she was just a babe, she flung open the door without knocking.

Rufus looked up in surprise, lit match and translucent green water pipe in his hands, the window flung open and the warm air acrid with the stench of pot. "Grr," he growled.

Jenny didn't even care. She'd always suspected he smoked pot, anyway. "Dad, I got into Waverly," she told him breathlessly. "You know, the boarding school I read about with the new art program? I got in!" she practically shouted at him. "I got in!"

Rufus blew out the match, opened his desk drawer, and chucked the evidence into it. Then he opened his arms to give her a big bear hug.

"I just wanted it so badly, it had to happen," Jenny gushed, her face pressed into his warm, smoky shoulder.

We've always been told, "Be careful what you wish for." But maybe Blair had it right after all: The more you want, the more you get.

Disclaimer: All the real names of places, people, and events have been altered or abbreviated to protect the innocent. Namely, me.

hey people!

Our last night together

We're now officially high school graduates!!! Let's get ready to party hearty—at the Yale Club!! There's no guest list and no dress code, so crashers—you may not be guaranteed a room, but you're certainly welcome! Definition of a crasher: anyone who did not graduate today and/or anyone who doesn't actually know the girl hosting the party.

Their last night together

Alas, **B**'s lovely English lord is flying home tomorrow. Will he break off his engagement to the girl it's rumored he's been betrothed to since he was a wee lad? Or will he marry her, leaving **B** in the lurch? At least she can drive off into the sunset in her new, adorable, bisque-colored convertible Beamer. Did you see it parked outside Brick Church? Imported directly from the Continent. No one—and I mean no one—in this country has that car.

Your e-mail

 Dear GG,
I'm a premed sophomore at Yale and I heard that kid **N** has already signed up to be a lab rat for the medical school's psychiatric division. Like, they're going to give him all these mind-altering drugs that they're trying out, and they even pay him to take them.
—jrmed

A: Dear jrmed,
Like he needs to be paid?! Anyway, first things first—the boy doesn't even have his high school diploma yet.
—GG

Q: Dear Gossip Girl,
My son tells me you are the voice of the young people and so I must ask if you know a gifted poet who was on his way to Evergreen College but tripped over his heart. You see, I am something of a poet myself! This poet was going to assist me with my history of sex poetry book, but he writes to say he doesn't come. I am upset! I need talented assistance! Maybe you can come to Olympia to help me. You sleep in hammock. My son makes good Greek food!
—professorpop

A: Dear professorpop,
My, is it ever tempting, but I kind of already have plans this summer. Besides, hammocks have never been my thing—I'm a 600-thread-count-Egyptian-cotton-sheet sort of girl. Your book sounds quite intriguing, though. Good luck with that.
—GG

They finally caught on

Almost all the private schools in Manhattan have finally figured it out: Seniors don't want to take final exams or sit in class the last month of school, nor do they need to, since they've already been accepted at college and are so mentally spent by then, they can't possibly learn anything new. So, starting next year, seniors will only have to go to class until the middle of May. They'll finish up the year by doing an internship of their choice anywhere in the city. Sounds pretty cool, huh? Too bad none of *us* got to do it. I could have "interned" with an online news column and "gone to work" in bed in my favorite black cotton DKNY intimates nightgown. Not that I'm bitter. After all, *I've already graduated!!!!*

Sightings

B mooning the **Yale Club** out of her new Beamer convertible. **V** mooning the Yale Club out of **B**'s new Beamer convertible. The girls started celebrating early, so who knows what kind of shape they'll be in later tonight. . . . That conceited indie film director paying a personal visit to **S**'s family's Fifth Avenue penthouse. **S** stepping out of her apartment building, looking resplendent in a yellow eyelet **Tocca** sundress. Thank goodness she changed. **J** in **Bed, Bath and Beyond**, already decorating her room at **Waverly Prep**. **D** buying a whole bucketful of red roses for guess who? Good thing she didn't leave town, but too bad she's forgotten all about him! Tonight should be *très, très intéressant*.

See you then!

You know you love me.

gossip girl

it was the best of times, it was the worst of times

Still wearing her perfectly fitted white satin Oscar de la Renta suit, Blair sat on Lord Marcus's knee on a brown leather wing-back chair in the Yale Club lounge, feeling weirdly content as throngs of people wandered into her graduation party with their yearbooks tucked under their arms. She and Lord Marcus hadn't had a chance to consummate her graduation *yet*, but as soon as the party kicked into high gear, they'd slip up to her suite and do it once and for all. She'd already filled the suite with Diptyque candles in scents of sandalwood, bergamot, and lime, and underneath her suit she was wearing her favorite new cream-colored embroidered cotton Cosabella camisole-and-thong set.

The lounge was its same crusty old New York self, except for the six flat-screen Pioneer TVs hanging from the wood-paneled walls, running Vanessa's latest film on a constant loop. The fact that all the characters in the film were slowly trickling into the party made it seem like the opening night of an edgy new documentary, and everyone at the party felt totally famous.

"I told you I was telegenic," Chuck Bass crowed, watching himself onscreen. He'd arrived with an entourage of crew-cutted boys in gray flannel uniforms no one else there had ever laid eyes on before.

That's because he'd raided the sophomore class of some random Catholic school near his Sutton Place apartment and paid the boys to come.

"They're cute," Isabel remarked, eyeballing a particularly innocent, wide-eyed-looking boy who was signing Chuck's Riverside Prep yearbook with a yellow highlighter pen. Isabel had changed into a pair of cutoff Rogan jeans and a cut-up red Juicy Couture T-shirt and was looking almost indecently slutty.

The boy eyeballed her back. He'd never seen so much well-tended exposed skin. Maybe it was his lucky night!

"They're only, like, thirteen years old," Kati scoffed as she flipped through her yearbook, counting how many people had signed it. She was saving her virginity for college. Sort of. Technically she'd already lost it to Chuck Bass at a party at Serena's house, like, two years ago, but she'd been so drunk at the time, she didn't even remember it.

Lord Marcus slipped something cool and wonderful around Blair's neck. Blair touched her collarbone and glanced down. It was a Bvlgari pearl choker exactly like the one she'd borrowed from her mother for her *Breakfast at Fred's* audition, only ten times nicer. Each pearl in the strand was its own unique shape, imperfect and perfect at the same time, fastened by an ornate gold clasp shaped like the letter *B*. "Congratulations, Bee," he murmured, kissing her on the nape of the neck.

Bee?

Blair had always wanted a nickname. She tilted her chin up to kiss him on the mouth, feeling drunk with happiness and all the vodka she'd consumed with Vanessa in the hours between graduation and now. She had an insanely cute new car, an insanely hot new boyfriend, and she was going to Yale in the fall. The pearls were just accessories for her already-perfect life.

Well, aren't we smug?

"I'd love for you to come to England this summer," Lord Marcus whispered, his lips brushing Blair's hair. "My family's desperate to meet you. You could stay at the house. And maybe we could even fly to Paris and see your dad while you're over."

Blair's breath caught in her throat and she turned around, blinking up at him like a vacant cartoon princess who'd just been woken from a witch's spell. He'd only asked her to visit him, but it had sounded almost like . . . *a marriage proposal.* He was her prince, her knight—well, not exactly, but a lord was almost the same thing. He'd swooped in on his white stallion, swept her off her feet, and now he wanted to take her home to meet his parents because soon—maybe even sometime this summer—he was going to give her an incredibly rare diamond ring, kneel down before her, and ask her to marry him.

Not that he actually mentioned marriage. And when exactly did a white stallion enter the picture?

"Yes," Blair responded blissfully. "Oh, yes!"

It was more of a response to the marriage proposal in her head than to Lord Marcus's original proposal, but in the world according to Blair, they were intrinsically linked: She would go to England and she would come back engaged to Lord Marcus.

Even though she was only seventeen and her mom had never even met him. Not that she ever planned to purposely introduce her mother to Marcus. They could meet at the wedding. Or maybe they'd elope to some remote South Pacific island and have an intimate nighttime wedding on a beach with only the natives as their witnesses. They'd eat fire-roasted goat and dance barefoot in the sand.

Remember, anything can happen on the Island of Blair.

She'd kept her summer open, thinking she would need all two and a half months just to shop and pack for Yale. She'd even considered going over to Europe to see her dad—but mostly to shop, because the stores in New York never put out any fall fashions until September, and she had to be in New Haven for orientation at the end of August. How on earth would she arrive at Yale with the right cashmere sweaters, ankle boots, and fitted jackets unless she bought them directly from Prada in Milan or Burberry in London?

Now her summer was more defined. She would shop, get engaged, and then shop some more.

"I can't bear to think this is our last night together," Marcus lamented, kissing her behind the ear. "It would do my heart good to know you're going to come over in a couple of weeks."

Blair would have closed her eyes and kissed him and then whispered something about how she really, really needed to lie down so would he please walk her to her suite so she could rip his clothes off and they could consummate their marriage a little early, but then Serena and Nate wandered into the party behind a group of L'École girls who were all smoking Gauloises and wearing crocheted Marni halter tops and gold Gucci toe-ring sandals because that French model, Pru, had just worn a crocheted Marni halter top and gold Gucci toe-ring sandals on the cover of the June issue of French *Vogue*. Serena had changed her outfit—luckily. Otherwise Blair would have broken her perfect, aristocratic nose.

"I thought you told me they broke up," Tina Ford, who'd just graduated from Seaton Arms, commented to Isabel Coates. She bit into an Absolut Citron–soaked ice cube. "Isn't that why they both missed graduation?"

"I heard they were never really together," Kati Farkas trilled in reply, even though Tina wasn't even talking to her. "Nate's gay. He came out last week. And he's in so much trouble. His parents are disowning him. They're not even going to pay for Yale."

"So why is Serena still pretending to go out with him?" Isabel demanded, lifting up her ripped red T-shirt and exposing her tummy just to give that innocent-looking Catholic school boy Chuck had brought with him a little thrill.

The other girls rolled their eyes. "Oh, you know how she is. She always has to be so *nice* to everybody," Rain complained. "Nate's dad probably, like, *hired* her to flirt with Nate so he wouldn't be gay anymore!"

Actually, that does sound like something Captain Archibald would do.

As they'd filed out of Brick Church, and in the seconds before their families caught up with them, Serena had tried to explain to Blair why she'd almost missed graduation, while Blair had pretended not to listen. Obviously Serena's second *Breakfast at Fred's* audition was way more important than listening to Blair's speech or getting her diploma. At least Blair had the satisfaction of knowing that Serena would never get the part. She was way too tall, too blond, and too blue-eyed—totally wrong for it.

"I got the part!" Serena screamed at the top of her lungs, so excited, she didn't care who was listening. She grabbed Nate and squeezed him with her long, perfectly toned arms. "Ken Mogul just called. I got the part!"

Blair nearly fell off Lord Marcus's knee. She'd already been hating Serena all over again for missing her graduation speech and for wearing the exact same Oscar de la Renta suit she had. And of course she still secretly hated her for being with Nate. It hadn't seemed possible to hate her any more—until now. But Blair had already started talking to Serena again—she'd even taken Serena's chemistry exam for her, for Christ's sake, so now she was stuck with the awkward choice of suddenly acting like a bitch for no reason in front of Lord Marcus, or being completely fake and pretending to be nice so Lord Marcus wouldn't think she was a bitch and change his mind about wanting to marry her.

As if he hadn't already noticed her bitchy side.

Nate stood next to Serena like a hired piece of celebrity

arm candy. He rubbed his eyes and smiled at Blair and Marcus blearily, and for the first time in a long time, Blair wondered what she'd ever seen in him. No matter how often they broke up, her happily-ever-after fantasies had always featured Nate, but now they had a new and improved co-star. She leaned back against Marcus's chest, making it very clear that she was supremely comfortable on his lap and totally unruffled by Serena's news. Her perfectly tailored suit was a little warm in the stuffy room, but it looked so good on her, she didn't care.

All of a sudden, another good-looking but shorter couple stepped around Nate and Serena and gazed tensely around the room, as if they were worried someone might yell at them for crashing the party. Blair sat up and unbuttoned her Oscar de la Renta suit jacket, flinging it onto the floor in disgust. The male part of the new couple was her twelve-year-old brother Tyler, attempting to look like a rock star by wearing a vintage Armani tuxedo jacket over a ripped black AC/DC T-shirt. The dimple-cheeked, waiflike girl on his arm was wearing the same fucking white Oscar de la Renta suit Blair was. She was even wearing the same fucking Manolo Blahnik shoes as Blair. Her fucking hair was the same color as Blair's, and it was cut in a short layered bob, just like Blair's. Blair squinted. She had never seen this fucking girl in her life, but if she wasn't mistaken, she was also wearing Chanel's fucking Stroppy lip gloss, Blair's fucking favorite.

Growl.

Blair hitched up the straps on her totally see-though cream-colored Cosabella camisole. If it hadn't been for Lord Marcus, she'd have grabbed the girl by the scruff of the neck and thrown her out on the street.

"Hey, sis," Tyler greeted her in a fake stoner voice, puffing up his shoulders in an attempt to look bigger. "This is Jasmine. Jazz, this is my sister, Blair."

"Cool," Blair's apple-cheeked clone responded casually.

Like she hadn't just spent all day trying to dress exactly like Blair.

Blair wrinkled up her pert little nose. "I got the part!" she heard Serena scream from the other side of the room, for what seemed like the thousandth fucking time. She picked up her cigarette holder, waiting for Marcus to give her a light. "How do you do?" she replied in her best gracious-under-pressure Audrey Hepburn imitation, blowing smoke over her brother's and his stupid little girlfriend's heads.

Serena may well have gotten the part, but Blair *lived* it, every day.

nothing can keep us together

It was almost surreal how graduation changed everything and everybody. The party was like being at a reunion, except that they'd only just graduated that morning. Some of the girls were still wearing their white graduation dresses with rubber flip-flops and their hair all undone, looking like runaway brides. The boys had rolled the cuffs up on their neatly pressed khakis, and their school ties hung askew on their bare, sun-kissed chests, so that they resembled models in a Ralph Lauren menswear campaign, dressed up for cocktails but sitting on a dock with their feet dangling in a lake as if they'd rather drink beers together than go back inside to the stuffy cocktail party.

Serena thought of herself as an emotional person. The fashion designer Les Best had even named a perfume Serena's Tears when he'd caught her weeping in the snow at a photo shoot in Central Park. She'd always thought she'd be a basket case during graduation. After all, she'd grown up with these people, shared the same ups and downs, suffered the same disappointments and triumphs. But here she was, nothing short of ecstatic. Even Nate's mopey, distracted disposition couldn't bring her down, because *she'd gotten the part!*

Yes, we heard her the first time.

In his usual pretentious, oddball manner, Ken Mogul

hadn't even watched her second audition. He'd kept his back turned, trying to ascertain whether she radiated the right energy for the part. When she finished delivering her lines, he didn't turn around, just held up his hand and said, "Thank you."

The second audition had taken place in an old warehouse in the Meatpacking District, on the opposite end of Manhattan from Brick Church. Serena was already dressed for graduation, and she'd promised to pay her taxi driver handsomely if he waited for her outside. Within seconds, she was hurtling east on Fourteenth Street, praying that Mrs. M wouldn't make her repeat her senior year and realizing too late that she'd left her shoes behind.

After graduation, over lunch at Tavern on the Green, her mom had been more miffed over the missing white Jimmy Choos than the fact that Serena had nearly skipped the ceremony. "What kind of girl goes around barefoot?" Mrs. van der Woodsen wanted to know. Then Ken Mogul had called Serena's cell.

"I don't like tans or freckles, so please, try and stay out of the sun. We start shooting at Fred's next month," he announced gruffly. Serena just sat there with the phone pressed against her ear, trying to figure out what he was talking about. Then she realized: *I got the part. I got the part!*

Hello? Can we change the subject now please?

Her parents considered acting in movies somewhat déclassé, but less than nine months after getting kicked out of boarding school, Serena had been accepted at Yale, Harvard, Brown, and Princeton and was about to star in a remake of *Breakfast at Tiffany's*. They could hardly complain.

I got the part, I got the part! Serena kept screaming to herself. Her first real part in her first real movie. For the first time in her life she realized that this was something she really *wanted*. And it hadn't just happened. She'd *made* it happen. Good thing she was now at a party, because there was an excited little girl on a trampoline inside her, bouncing and bouncing and bouncing.

Boing!

"I heard she and Ken Mogul went on a drug binge last night and she totally talked him into giving her the lead in his movie. He was all set to skew it older and cast Natalie Portman, but Serena brainwashed him," someone whispered.

"She even tried to get him to cast Nate as her costar, but he's always so baked, he forgot his lines during his tryout," whispered someone else.

"And didn't you hear? Nate totally didn't graduate. He got busted for stealing painkillers from the nurse's office at his school, and now he has to go to some drug rehab prison thing in the *bad* part of the Hamptons, like, *all summer,*" Rain Hoffstetter informed all who would listen. She'd hooked up with Charlie Dern when their parents had parked next to each other at a drive-in movie theater out on the Cape last weekend. They'd been talking on the phone every night since, so she was very up-to-date on her Nate information.

Nate was grateful for his role as Serena's mute piece of arm candy. He felt like he'd been encased in six inches of clear plastic. Everyone's voice sounded muffled and distant. It didn't help that Blair looked radiant on Marcus's knee, or that Serena clearly didn't need a boyfriend right now, or that he was incredibly stoned.

"Blair?! Did you hear? I got the part!" Serena threw herself at Blair and Lord Marcus, dragging Nate along with her. She squeezed Blair's shoulders exuberantly. "You're not mad, are you?"

Me, mad? Blair smiled tensely, still intent on impressing Marcus with her sweet, forgiving nature.

Ha!

"You're such an excellent actress," she finally told her ex-friend politely. "You totally deserve it."

Serena's ear-to-ear smile faded slightly. She knew Blair too well not to be able to gauge that she was less than pleased and more than pissed. Blair was complicated: It was best to flee when she was acting volatile. "Is Vanessa around? I can't wait to tell her—I'm totally talking to Ken Mogul about hiring her to film the movie!"

Her face resolutely blank, Blair pointed to where Vanessa was sitting in the corner with her own personal bottle of Stoli, happily signing the yearbooks of all the nonseniors at the party who thought she was beyond cool.

"Vanessa Marigold Abrams!" Serena cried and dashed across the room, leaving Nate behind.

Nate stood in front of Blair and Lord Marcus all cuddled up in their wing-back chair, his hands in his pockets, feeling like a jerk.

"How's it feel?" Lord Marcus asked, reaching up to shake Nate's hand.

Nate didn't know who knew about his graduation predicament, and he didn't much want to talk about it. "I'm just glad it's over," he mumbled. Lord Marcus looked bigger than he remembered, and even though he was a guy, Nate could appreciate how handsome he was. Blair had really scored.

"That's how I feel," Blair agreed with a perky smile. She reached up and casually stroked the back of Lord Marcus's tanned, muscular neck, showing off how comfortable she was talking to Nate while sitting on Marcus's lap.

Nate suddenly perked up, remembering the reason he'd come to the party in the first place. "Blair, can I talk to you for a minute?" he asked, although to him it sounded like he'd said, "Woo shee ga ga?"

Blair had always been the needy one in their on-again-off-again relationship, so it was a new experience to see Nate hovering over her, looking uncomfortable and a little desperate, with something bulky stuffed under his arm. Was he going to give her a present? she wondered. God knew she'd given him enough presents in their time together, and he'd hardly given her anything except flowers a few times, when he'd thought of it.

"Don't go anywhere. We'll be right back," she murmured to Marcus. She slipped off his knee, flashing him a sultry I'm-only-tolerating-this-party-for-a-half-hour-more-before-I-tear-your-clothes-off look. Then she followed Nate into a semiquiet corner of the crowded room, trying to appear impatient and indifferent while her heart thundered so furiously in her chest, she wouldn't have been surprised if it were visible through her nearly transparent cream-colored camisole.

Nate pulled the thing out from under his arm—a navy blue paper Gap shopping bag, folded in half. Blair was slightly appalled. He'd bought her a gift at the Gap?

"Here," he murmured, yanking something out of the bag and handing it to her. Blair recognized it at once: the moss green cashmere V-neck sweater she'd given him over a year ago.

"But you love this sweater," she complained, feeling for the gold heart she'd sewn into the left sleeve before she gave it to him so he would always be wearing her heart on his sleeve. It wasn't there. Blair felt inside the right sleeve, although she was absolutely positive she'd sewn it into the left. Nope. Where the fuck was it?

"I just don't think it'd be right to keep it," Nate replied solemnly. He blinked hard, willing the tears not to fall. He wondered if Blair even remembered the gold heart, which was now sitting in a sailboat-shaped blue-and-green sea glass ashtray beside his bed, a constant reminder of their failed relationship.

Hey, maybe he should talk to Les Best about a new men's cologne—Nate's Tears!

"It's just a sweater," Blair insisted, feeling completely confused. Why couldn't Nate just be normal and give her a boring Tiffany chain-link bracelet or something to congratulate her on graduating? Was this his way of saying sorry, or that he wanted her back? Well, it was a little late for that. "Please, keep it."

"I can't," Nate gasped, choking up. He wished he could confide in Blair, tell her all about how he'd screwed up graduating; how he'd screwed up in general. But Nate had never truly confided in Blair, and now probably wasn't the best time to start.

"Fine." She folded the sweater neatly and placed it on a Yale-blue-upholstered armchair nearby. She put her hands on her hips, determined not to allow herself to waver. She had a new boyfriend now. A much, much better one. "Was that all?"

Nate nodded. Then he took a step forward, closed his emerald green eyes, and placed a careful kiss on Blair's smooth, soft cheek. He opened his eyes. "Congratulations," he murmured before turning away.

Blair stood there for a moment with her arms folded across her chest, ignoring the stares of her whispering classmates. *It's just a sweater*, she repeated silently to herself.

Yeah. Right.

remind me how much i love you

Dan kept his hunter green Riverside Prep school tie on for Blair's party. He wanted to look his handsomest when he announced to Vanessa that he'd deferred admission to Evergreen and wanted to spend next year and possibly the rest of his life with her. As soon as they arrived at the party, Jenny went right to the bar to score a glass of champagne, but Dan lingered by the door, his arms full of red roses, transfixed by the sight of Vanessa looking resplendent in her sexy low-cut white graduation dress and funky white wedge-heeled shoes. There was a pink flush to her cheeks and a sparkle to her dark brown eyes as she chatted with Serena van der Woodsen. Serena was gorgeous as usual, with her mane of pale blond hair cascading between her bare shoulder blades and her endless legs, but the sight of her didn't turn Dan on the way the sight of Vanessa did.

"Hey, hot stuff, get your ass over here!" Vanessa shouted at him from across the room. She'd been drunk since one o'clock in the afternoon and the sight of Dan, his arms full of roses, was less a turn-on than a revelation. A drunken one.

This morning she'd almost driven off with the wrong boy. It was Dan she loved. How could she not—with his scruffy looks, his painfully wrought poems, and the way he kept showing up unexpectedly on her roof with his clothes off.

As Dan approached, she sort of oofed herself out of the Yale-blue-and-white striped wing-back chair she was sitting in but then gave up and fell back into it again. "I'm trying to hug you," she explained, laughing at herself.

She's drunk, he realized.

Serena grabbed him and kissed him on the cheek, then pushed him into Vanessa's lap. "You're always so cute," she cooed, ruffling Dan's scraggly light brown hair as red roses fell out of his arms and scattered around their feet.

Vanessa tickled him under the arms and he shrugged her needling fingers away, suddenly feeling more like someone's cute four-year-old brother than Vanessa's stud-muffin boyfriend.

"So, the big news is Serena's going to be a movie star, and I'm going to help make her cheesy big-budget movie, because if we sell out, we'll make selling out look cool," Vanessa told him with drunken excitement.

Serena and Vanessa slapped each other five like old soccer teammates. Then Serena refilled her glass of Dom out of the magnum on the floor next to Vanessa's chair and handed the overflowing flute to Dan. "To Hollywood," she cried gleefully, waiting for Dan to chug it down.

Dan perched on Vanessa's pale bare knee, trying not to spill his champagne. He'd prepared a Pablo Neruda love poem to recite, but maybe now wasn't such a great time.

"Do you think I should tell them to turn the music up so we can dance?" Serena burped loudly.

"Definitely." Vanessa bounced up and down on the chair cushion, causing Dan to tumble onto the floor. "Dan will dance with us, won't you, Dan?"

Dan clambered to his feet, eager for Serena to leave him alone with Vanessa. "Sure."

Serena whirled away, a vision of yellow silk and golden hair. The room was packed with people and the air was thick with cigarette smoke and perfume. Everyone had been celebrating since morning, so it felt like four A.M. instead of ten P.M. For old times' sake, a group of girls from Seaton Arms and Constance were playing Spin the Bottle with a group of boys from Riverside.

"Me first!" Chuck Bass crowed, kneeling down to give the empty Stoli bottle an energetic spin.

Typical.

"Dad got pretty mad at me today," Dan confessed. He perched on the arm of Vanessa's chair, suddenly so nervous, he couldn't drink his champagne. She wasn't looking at him, but he hoped she was listening. "I guess I should've told him before I made my speech."

Vanessa was watching Serena as she flirted with Jarvis Cocker—the crazy cool British DJ wearing a black top hat at his station across the room. She had to admire how completely shameless Serena was. She'd do anything as long as it wasn't too illegal or humiliating, just because it amused her. The thing Vanessa most admired, though, was that Serena wasn't conceited—she was just *Serena*. And she didn't seem to need anyone else to be Serena. She was just fine being herself.

"See, I kind of changed my mind about going to Evergreen," Dan continued. "At least, not right away."

Vanessa could feel Dan staring at her and she realized he was trying to tell her something important and that she'd missed half of it. "Wait. What?"

Dan slid off the arm of the chair and knelt down on the burnished amber wood floor, grasping her hands in his. *"I do not love you except because I love you,"* he recited.

Vanessa was glad the room was so crowded; otherwise she might have been a little embarrassed.

"I can't imagine not sharing the air you breathe, living all those miles away," Dan told her earnestly, in his own words this time. "Like I said in my speech, I can go to college any time, but I'm in love with you now. And the only thing I want, my only requirement, is to be with you."

Vanessa's face turned hot and prickly. Yes, she loved him, but did he have to be so darned dramatic? "So you're . . ." Her voice trailed off uncertainly.

"Staying here," Dan filled in, gazing up at her with adoring brown eyes. "With you."

All of a sudden that new OutKast song that no one could listen to without jumping to their feet and wiggling their ass came blasting out of the speakers ten decibels louder than the smooth R&B that had been playing before. Serena bounded over, grabbed Vanessa's hand, and pulled her out of the chair. "Come on, groovy girl," she coaxed. "Show me what you got."

Vanessa had always loathed dancing, at least in public, but she needed to get away from Dan right now, and all his intensity. Serena bumped hips with her and Vanessa laughed and bumped her back. She could feel Dan watching them intently, but she didn't turn around. The music was good, and she felt vibrant and beautiful in her slippery, shimmering white Morgane Le Fay dress. Dan must have been crazy to think not going to college next year was a good idea. Of course he was going, but they could spend the summer together working it out. The music grew louder still, and Vanessa raised her bare arms in the air, grooving to it. Dan was completely nuts, but so was she for ever having said she didn't dance.

n's trail of tears

Nate sat on the edge of one of the Yale Club lounge's oriental carpets, pretending to watch the Spin the Bottle game. That French hippie chick, Lexie, who'd followed him around for a few weeks claiming to be madly in love with him, and her other L'École friends were sitting in a tight circle only a few feet away, all wearing crocheted halter tops with their skinny bellies showing, smoking Gauloises like fiends. He hoped she wouldn't notice him.

Too late.

"Nate?" Lexie sat up on her haunches, her scrawny, tan tummy bulging in a way she must have thought was irresistible. She'd gotten a navel piercing, and it was still pink and new.

Ew.

She stretched her long bare arms overhead, giving the rest of the room a fine view of the sun, moon, and stars tattoo on her right shoulder blade.

Ooh la la.

Nate smiled, pretending to have only just noticed her. "Hey, Lexie." He waved cautiously and then hugged his knees to show that he had no intention of joining her.

Lexie rolled her dark brown eyes and flipped her long raven-colored ponytail over one shoulder. "Bastard," she retorted with a heavy French accent and a very French-looking scowl. "You broke my heart."

Something exciting had just happened in the Spin the Bottle game, and everyone whooped and clapped. Nate began to clap, too—anything to avoid a confrontation with Lexie.

Serena and that weird shaven-headed girl from Constance who Blair was supposedly living with and reportedly having a lesbian affair with were dancing like disco diva freaks in the middle of the room, looking drunk and ecstatic—the way you were supposed to look the day you graduated from high school.

If, that is, you actually obtained your diploma that day, unlike a certain person we know.

Nate had a sudden flash of déjà vu, or maybe it was ennui. At any rate, it was something sad that sounded French. He remembered being drunk at a random party at that guy Dan Humphrey's house over on the West Side back in ninth or tenth grade and letting Blair and Serena draw a face on his bare stomach with a black indelible marker. They'd named the face Buck Naked, and each girl had kissed Buck repeatedly over the course of the evening, even after Nate passed out.

Those were the days.

Suddenly Nate became filled with dread. What if he'd already had all the fun he was ever going to have? What if it was all downhill from here?

And what if he'd gotten more and more stupid with each year of high school instead of smarter? That can happen when you remain stoned most of your life.

Tears began to ooze slowly down his golden cheeks. Everybody else at the party seemed so happy and so excited about their future, but he wasn't really sure what he had to look forward to anymore.

j considers losing it before boarding school

Parties had always seemed intimidating to Jenny—especially parties where the majority of the girls were normal-chested and taller, prettier, and more confident than she was. But now that she was into boarding school, Jenny felt like the possibilities—at least, the possibilities for *her*—were multitudinous. She didn't have to be tiny little Jenny Humphrey, the curly-haired artistic girl with the knobby knees and gigantic boobs. Next year at Waverly she could be Jennifer Humphrey, the outrageously confident boy magnet, coolest girl in the sophomore class, or maybe even the whole school.

Maybe.

And if she was going to change her image, it seemed prudent that she do something drastic, like lose her virginity.

Whoa.

She'd been watching Nate Archibald for a while now. He seemed different than when he'd broken her heart on New Year's Eve. He was crying, for one thing, and his shoulders were slumped, like he'd gotten some bad news and hadn't been able to shake it. Even the glitter seemed to have left his emerald green eyes. She could hardly resist the urge to give him a hug.

"Hi, Nate," she squeaked, boldly touching him on the shoulder. "Remember me?"

With that chest? Even the stonedest boy could hardly forget.

Nate scrubbed his hands over his blotchy face and attempted a smile. "Howdy, Jennifer," he greeted her, with the sort of tired cheerfulness of someone who's had kind of a rough day and doesn't much feel like talking.

"So you're all done with school and everything?" Jenny persisted. She was acutely aware that from his angle Nate was looking up at the shelflike undersides of her gigantic breasts, which were stuffed into a stretchy black Anthropologie halter top with a built-in Lycra bra. He probably couldn't even see her face. She squatted down beside him, teetering slightly on her baby blue BCBG kitten-heel slides. "I'm going to boarding school at Waverly Prep next year," she blurted out. "I totally can't wait!"

Nate was sort of surprised that Jennifer wanted to talk to him at all, but he was grateful because it meant he didn't have to avoid talking to Lexie anymore. "That's a good school."

"Yeah, and I don't ever have to wear a stupid Constance uniform again," Jenny added excitedly, already regretting how petulant and childish she sounded. Then she remembered something that wouldn't make her sound childish at all. She inched a little closer to Nate's ear. He smelled like freshly laundered shirt and that heart-stoppingly delicious Hermès cologne he always wore. "I have a tab of E in my bag. Someone gave it to me at the Croton School when I was visiting. I don't even know if we can even split one tab, but . . ." She smiled her coyest come-hither smile.

What a flirt, what a risk-taker the new, on-her-way-to-boarding-school Jenny Humphrey was!

Nate blinked. Jennifer wasn't just talking to him, she was flirting with him—*hard*. What, did she think he'd just gulp down a tab of E and hook up with her right in the middle of the Yale Club lounge, surrounded by everyone he knew, including his ex-girlfriend Blair and his he-wasn't-really-sure-but-he-figured-she-was-probably-soon-to-be-ex-girlfriend Serena?

Had that ever stopped him before?

Nate had only taken Ecstasy a couple of times with Charlie, Anthony, and Jeremy, but both times he'd enjoyed himself immensely. There was nothing like that good, groovy, E feeling—until it wore off and you were tired and dehydrated and just wanted to float in a bucket of Poland Spring. He was definitely feeling lower right now than he ever had in his entire life. Maybe a little E with little Jennifer Humphrey—who seemed to be getting even cuter with age—was just what he needed.

Jenny could see that Nate was tempted. Empowered by her ability to snare hot older boys with her seductive ways, she breathed lustily into his ear. "Let's go into the bathroom and do it."

Hello? Does she not remember what happened the last time she was alone in a bathroom with a horny older boy?

what you choose not to hear can't hurt you

Blair was in a stall in one of the Yale Club's pristine and elegant gold-accented ladies' rooms, wondering at the fact that she hadn't made herself sick in over a month, when she heard the first worrying rumors.

"I heard he wasn't even a real lord. He's just this English guy who came over here and pretended to be this big aristocrat. I bet he doesn't go on fox hunts or wear a top hat and tails to dinner or anything like that," Laura Salmon blathered from the stall next to Blair's.

"I just think it's really shitty of him. I mean, if he's engaged to some girl in England, that means he's actually cheating on both of them," Kati Farkas replied carelessly as she spritzed her hair with a sample-size bottle of Frederick Fekkai hairspray for the third time that night. "I just love the way this stuff smells. Don't you love the way it smells? I even put it on my clothes sometimes, even though I know that's kind of gross. I mean, it's hairspray!"

Blair kept the pleated satin skirt of her white Oscar de la Renta suit hitched up so the girls wouldn't recognize it. *Were they talking about Lord Marcus?*

"I just think someone should tell her," Laura declared before flushing. She pushed the stall door open and began to wash her hands with the L'Occitane lemon peel foam hand wash provided by the Yale Club. "Don't you?"

"Totally," Kati agreed.

Like they'd ever have the nerve.

Blair waited until they'd gone before pushing open the stall door. Her stomach was roiling from all the vodka and champagne she'd drunk in the last few hours, but she wasn't about to resort to puking and risk splattering the skirt of her exquisite suit.

What do they know about Marcus? she fumed. Their petty jealousy was so transparent, it made her even more nauseous just thinking about it. Of course he was a lord. Hadn't they noticed his wonderful scuff-free Church's shoes? The flawless way his hair was cut? The tailor-made seams of his Savile Row shirts? Hadn't they heard the way he called her "gorgeous" and "darling" and kissed her hand like it was the most natural thing in the world? There'd been no mention of a fiancée when Blair had Googled him. No fucking way was he engaged—to anyone but her. She closed her eyes dreamily. Lady Blair Rhodes—it did have a nice ring to it.

The bathroom door swung open and Isabel Coates marched in, looking frazzled because her white satin Dior hair clip had come loose while she was dancing. Isabel was always such a freak about her hair, Blair wondered why she didn't just cut it all off.

"Oh. You're in here," Isabel observed, making it obvious that she'd just been part of Kati's and Laura's ongoing dissection of the so-called Lord Marcus. "I guess I should be the one to tell you." She lowered her voice to let Blair know that what she had to tell her was extremely important. "Before you get hurt."

Like she actually cared?

Blair narrowed her blue eyes, glaring icily at Isabel's reflection in the gilt-framed mirror. "Tell me what?"

Isabel tucked a few stray brown hairs behind her ears, then frowned and ripped out the hair clip, starting all over again.

Blair thought her cutoff jeans and ripped red Juicy T-shirt made her look tacky and desperate, like Paris Hilton.

"That Lord Marcus guy is married," Isabel told her matter-of-factly, wincing with effort as she tried to get her ponytail completely smooth and lump-free.

Blair smeared Chanel Stroppy lip gloss over her lips for the seventh time in five minutes. She was so mad, she thought she just might throw up after all. "*Bullshit.*"

Isabel rolled her curly-lashed brown eyes and sighed as if she were already totally bored with the subject matter. "Well, *almost*. He's engaged. He's been engaged since he was, like, ten years old. You know, like Lady Diana and Prince Charles?"

Blair spun away from the mirror, her fists clenched tightly to keep from strangling Isabel's ostrichlike neck. "And where exactly did you hear that?"

Isabel shrugged her shoulders maddeningly. "Everybody knows. It's, like, a *fact*."

Depending on your definition of the word *fact*.

"That's the stupidest—" Blair was about to try and defend Lord Marcus's honor, but she stopped herself. They were young, they were in love—who cared what anyone thought? Even if there *was* some boring girl back in England that Lord Marcus was supposed to marry, she probably looked like Queen Victoria and sat on her fat ass in her castle eating crumpets all day, wondering why Lord Marcus never called.

Isabel smiled at her reflection, finally satisfied. "I just thought you should know." She shrugged her shoulders and then cocked her overwaxed eyebrows at Blair. "Wanna come have a cigarette with us?" she offered, as if they were all still thirteen years old and only smoked in groups.

"No." Blair pushed past her and out the bathroom door. She peeked into the insanely crowded lounge, but the chair where she and Lord Marcus had been sitting together was now occupied by Nate's loud, stoned, skinny friend Jeremy and some skanky French girl trying to teach him how to blow heart-shaped smoke rings. Lord Marcus was nowhere to be seen. Blair fingered the Bvlgari pearl choker and teetered down the hall to the elevator.

All night she'd wanted to get Lord Marcus alone in his suite. Now was her chance.

d rethinks his summer plans

Dan's cigarette hand shook violently as he watched his sister disappear into the men's room, followed by that arrogant stoner prince of the Upper East Side, Nate Archibald. Jenny seemed to be getting bolder and more self-assured as the year progressed, while he seemed to be regressing back to the girl-less, friendless loser he'd been up until this year. She'd even wrangled her way into boarding school way after admissions for next year were closed, while he'd whittled his options down to nothing.

The music was really loud now, and Vanessa and Serena had inspired half the room to get up and dance. Vanessa had kicked off her wedge-heeled shoes, baring her black-polished toes and pale, deeply arched feet. Dan loved to kiss the arches of her feet. He could write sonnets about the arches of her feet. But that was back when Vanessa didn't drink or dance or wear white or anything but black jeans, black kneesocks, and Doc Martens. She seemed so different now—if he were to write a poem about her, he wasn't sure where he'd begin.

Vanessa danced over to him and snaked her arms around his neck. Her pale skin was slick was sweat and her eyelids were heavy from all the vodka she'd consumed. "I do love you, Dan. I really do," she breathed hotly into his ear before shimmying away again, her whole body aglow. Dan stared after her, honestly believing that she did love him. She just didn't need him with her—not all the time. She was too busy shedding her lumpy black cocoon and transforming into a shimmering, white-winged moth.

But he'd already deferred his admission at Evergreen. What was he supposed to do now?

Lighting a Camel, he thought about barging into the men's room to rescue Jenny just for old times' sake and because such a noble act might make him feel better, but he was sick of always being the responsible older brother. Why couldn't someone rescue *him* for a change?

Okay.

"Son? Can I talk to you for a moment?"

Dan dropped his cigarette on the burgundy-and-gold oriental carpet, nearly jumping out of his faded blue Vans sneakers in surprise. It was his dad, in his favorite purple cotton sweatpants and black Mets T-shirt, looking ruddy-cheeked from too much red wine.

"I guess," Dan responded slowly. The music in the lounge was absurdly loud. Dan led Rufus outside. Out on Vanderbilt Avenue, the air was steamy and the sidewalks glittered black. Across the street, Grand Central Station looked like a giant relic of the city's past. A metallic blue '77 Buick Skylark—another relic from the past—was parked outside the Yale Club, looking completely out of place. Two skinny L'École girls were sitting on the curb having a fight over who was prettier or who smoked Gauloises with more panache. Behind them, their gold Gucci toe-ring sandals lay discarded in a pile. Suddenly they started kissing.

"Jesus," Rufus muttered, tugging on his matted salt-and-pepper beard, which resembled a used Brillo pad.

"What, Dad?" Dan whined impatiently. It was kind of embarrassing standing outside the party with his father. He felt like he was eleven years old.

Rufus tucked his hands inside the stretched-out waistband

of his purple sweatpants and Dan flinched at how unattractive the gesture was.

"After you left you got a call from some raving Greek professor at Evergreen. First he was going nuts about how you were supposed to sleep in his hammock and eat grape leaves with him, but then he started waxing philosophical about how kids your age can't differentiate between sex and love. Apparently he's quite an expert on the subject.

"Anyway, I talked to him for a while, and what it came down to was, he's going to make them hold your place open for the fall a) because I asked him to and b) because he was supposed to be your advisor and he wants you to help him with his book and c) because we both like you, even though you're a knucklehead."

Dan resented his dad's fond, vaguely patronizing tone. "You can't tell me what to do," he countered, crossing his hands over his chest and sounding younger by the minute. "You can't."

"That's true," Rufus agreed. He gestured toward the funky vintage Buick parked outside the Yale Club. "But I already got you the car. The least you could do is let me teach you how to drive it this summer and then get the hell out of here."

Dan had read about epiphanies and written about epiphanies, but he'd never actually had one. He'd gotten into nearly every college he applied to. He'd had a poem published in the *New Yorker*. And what was he going to do next year—work at a bookstore or wait tables to keep busy while Vanessa was in class?

"I could take the summer to work things out," he allowed, unwilling to let his father think he could be that easily persuaded. He and Vanessa could spend the summer hanging out whenever she wasn't busy working on that movie and he wasn't busy driving around in that . . . chick magnet. Who knew? Maybe there'd be other girls to love besides Vanessa—

all he had to do was get his license and drive out west to find out.

Rufus reached out to clap him on the back, but Dan opened up his arms and gave his dad a hug. "This party was kind of lame anyway," he confessed.

Rufus grunted and led him over to the car, which was basking in its own coolness under a streetlamp near the curb. "Then how 'bout I give you your first driving lesson?"

Aw. Don't you just love happy endings?

sex, drugs, and rock'n'roll

Jenny latched the door to the handicapped stall in the men's room, unsure of whether to take off her clothes or fish the tab of E out of her purse. There was an impatient flare to Nate's nostrils but she wasn't sure which he wanted first, sex or drugs.

She unzipped her black LeSportsac with the white Persian cats on it and clicked open her matching change purse. "Here it is." She removed the tiny piece of Saran Wrap with the pill inside and carefully began to unfold it.

Nate peered over her shoulder. "Do you want to take it or should I?"

Jenny didn't want it, and he obviously did. "You take it." She held out her palm and Nate pinched the tab between his thumb and forefinger. He opened his mouth, closed his eyes, and stuck out his tongue, pressing the tab onto it before opening his eyes and closing his mouth again. Like that, he didn't look very hot, but Jenny was still intent on hooking up with him. This was her swan song, her last chance to forge her own memories and be remembered.

Oh, she'd be remembered all right.

"Does it taste like anything?" she asked, genuinely curious.

"Nope." Nate smiled. The more time he spent alone with Jennifer, the more he felt like his old self again. All she wanted was a little no-obligation, no-expectations end-of-the-year fun before she took off for boarding school or wherever the hell she was going this summer, and that was his specialty. He bent down and kissed her carefully on the lips, like he was biting into something that was still too hot to eat. "But you do."

Jenny loved the idea that she was using Nate, and the fact that he *wanted* her to use him gave her even more of a thrill. He stroked her curly brown hair and she tilted her chin up and gazed into his stunning green eyes. "Remember when I fell so in love with you?"

Nate smiled again and kissed her again. He did that for a while, smiling and kissing, smiling and kissing, like he was lapping up a delicious ice cream cone.

"You've got skin like . . . like . . . *petals*," Nate remarked as the E began to take effect. He rubbed the tip of his nose against her temple. "Grr."

Jenny giggled. It felt completely amazing to be this close and comfortable with Nate again. He was absurdly handsome, and being kissed by him felt really, really, *really* good. But Nate was beginning to trip, and she didn't want to lose her virginity to a boy who thought he was a Labrador puppy. She wouldn't.

Well, at least she had that much integrity.

Still, this was her last crazy night out before she flew to Prague for the summer. She wasn't quite ready for it to end.

Nate rubbed his chin against her carefully plucked dark brown eyebrows, and she lifted her chin to catch him in another long, hungry kiss. Her brother was always moaning about how much his life sucked. But she couldn't have disagreed more. It wasn't like she'd planned for life to be this thrilling. It just was; it really was.

nothing like a little mystery

"Marcus, darling?" Blair called tentatively through the molded white wooden door to Marcus's suite. She'd never actually called him "darling" out loud before, but it was becoming her favorite endearment. "Are you in there?"

She considered stripping down to only her Bvlgari pearls right there in the hallway, but the Yale Club was booked solid, and what if some bow-tie-wearing Yale professor saw her naked tonight and then she wound up having him in Intro to Law or another one of her freshman classes next year?

Well, it would certainly make the class more interesting.

"Marcus?" Blair pressed her ear against the door, listening for him. Nothing. She tried the knob. The door was unlocked. She pushed it open a few inches and stuck her head inside. "Marcus?" Still nothing. She pushed the door open all the way.

The drawers of the suite's antique oak armoire had been pulled open and a damp towel lay strewn on the bed. The air was heavy with steam and the scent of Marcus's Carolina Herrera for Men cologne. The closet door stood open. The cedar suit hangers were all bare. Marcus was gone.

Whoops.

Blair sat down heavily on the bed, feeling very much like the jilted but beautiful heroine in one of the epic films in her head that she'd temporarily stopped watching. She'd forgone her enormous Jackie O sunglasses, her signature Hermès head scarf, and her Burberry tea-length trench coat, because the heroine who was in love and part of a couple didn't need them. Now she wanted them back.

How had this happened? Was her only purpose in life to serve as a fuck-over mat for boys like Nate and Lord Marcus to wipe the soles of their lying, cheating Church's of London shoes on?

Her stomach churning, she stood up and rushed next door to her own suite, fully intending to make herself sick as soon as she reached the toilet. Propped up on the bureau was a large cream-colored envelope with the words *My Darling B* scrawled on it in Marcus's swirly script, and a small black velvet box with the word BVLGARI printed on it in gold. Blair resisted opening the box and tore open the envelope. Inside was a note from Marcus written on a matching cream-colored Crane's note card with LORD MARCUS BEATON-RHODES printed on it in Yale blue ink, along with a British Airways plane ticket.

Blair remained standing as she devoured the note, trying to ignore the small explosions in her stomach, like soap bubbles popping.

Dearest darling Blair, Bee, my bumblebee,

How could I have known when I planned a brief visit to New York after I finished up at Yale that I would meet a girl and fall in love? And not just any girl—you. It would be impossible to describe my feelings, so I dashed out and bought you two little somethings to go with the necklace. Promise me you'll wear them all when I see you next, which should be only a few weeks away if you'd be so kind as to get your gorgeousness on the flight I so presumptuously booked a ticket for—first class, of course. It's in two weeks, which gives you ample time to buy a whole new wardrobe, have a series of facials or tanning treatments, or whatever you do to keep yourself

*looking as stunning as you always do. Sorry for running out on you
like this, but it's your graduation-from-high-school party, the only
one you'll ever have, and I didn't want to put a damper on it by
saying good-bye. All right, I'm off. Please come to England. I shall
miss you.*

Love for always,
Marcus

Blair snatched the black velvet box off the white-painted
bureau and pried it open. Two perfect, enormous round
pearls glowed back at her, each dangling from a gold cursive
B—the earrings to match the necklace. She ripped out her
boring pearl studs and put in the Bvlgaris.

Bee. My bumblebee.

It seemed highly doubtful that Marcus was engaged to
some overweight, big-nosed, blue-blooded duchess if he'd
bought Blair a plane ticket to travel to England to meet his
mum. Judging from his impeccable stationery, Lord Marcus
was a bona fide lord, too. And judging from the note and the
plane ticket and the pearls, he truly loved her.

Opening the top drawer of the bureau, she tucked the
plane ticket alongside her favorite black La Perla demicup bra.

Contrary to popular belief, there's nothing like a mysterious departure to pique a girl's interest.

you know you love me

Serena's pale blond hair was matted with sweat and her yellow Tocca dress clung to her skin like wet tissue paper. She'd been dancing for an hour and she could barely stand up. Vanessa was leaning against the wall, chugging from a bottle of Perrier, her cheeks red with exertion. Serena joined her, grabbing the water out of her friend's hand and pouring it down her throat.

"You haven't seen Dan, have you?" Vanessa asked breathlessly. Now that she was finished dancing, it might be fun to find a quiet nook in the club somewhere and make out with Dan for a while.

"Nope," Serena remarked. The two girls surveyed the room, their eyes stinging with the salt from their sweat. A group of gray-uniform-wearing tenth-grade boys from some Catholic school were making a human pyramid with Chuck Bass on top, even though he weighed as much as all of them combined. One of the L'École girls had taken off her halter top and was dancing by herself in the corner, smoking a joint and strumming a guitar, a sun, moon, and stars tattoo standing out on her shoulder blade.

"This party is weird," Vanessa observed.

"Have you seen Nate?" Serena asked. She vaguely remembered arriving with him, but she hadn't seen him since. She squinted, half expecting to find Nate weeping at the bar, but she couldn't see him anywhere.

Blair stepped away from the bar, a fresh flute of bubbling champagne in her hand and a fresh cigarette dangling from the antique ebony-and-mother-of-pearl cigarette holder between her glossed lips, looking like a character out of an old movie. Serena pushed herself away from the wall and went over to her.

"I love your pearls."

Blair decided not to spit in Serena's face or scratch her dark blue eyes out. "They're from Marcus."

Serena nodded, about to say something about what an amazing guy Marcus was, but she was distracted. "You haven't seen Nate, have you?"

Blair took a long sip of champagne and blew smoke into the air. She'd been busy accepting gifts from her mysterious royal beau. She didn't have time to keep track of Nate's erratic whereabouts. "Not really."

Serena scanned the room with her eyes. "He's been acting strange," she remarked, chewing on her thumbnail. "Don't you think so?"

Again, Blair really didn't have an opinion on the subject. The moss green sweater was where she'd left it, folded on a chair nearby. "I guess," she allowed.

That tiny big-chested ninth grader Jenny Humphrey stepped out of the alcove where the men's room was, her curly dark hair slightly askew and her mouth red and swollen, as if from too much kissing. She paused and held out her hand, as if to a child. Then Nate appeared, looking happily disoriented. Jenny put her arm around his waist, and he turned and kissed her eagerly on the mouth, as if her lips were made of chocolate or something.

"Oh!" Serena exclaimed, as if she'd been pinched. She blinked her dark blue eyes, trying to ascertain whether she was truly hurt or just surprised. It had never felt right, her and Nate being together. And it would be better to be single this summer so she could focus on the film. At least now she wouldn't have to bother breaking up with him. Not that they'd ever really been together.

No, not really.

"Typical," Blair scoffed. She shook a Merit Ultra Light out of her pack and handed it to Serena. "Don't be mad. He can't help himself."

Serena took the cigarette and propped it between her lips, waiting for Blair to light it for her. "I'm not mad," she sighed, feeling relieved. For once, she and Blair were bonding over Nate instead of fighting over him. It was a welcome change. "So, will you loan me that for the movie?" She pointed at Blair's cigarette holder. "Although I'll probably set my ass on fire if I try to use it. I'm such a klutz."

Blair loved it when Serena put herself down. It gave her hope. "Of course I will."

Instinctively the two girls turned as someone careened toward them from across the room. Nate's face was slack, his green eyes were huge, and his body seemed more loose-limbed than usual. He came at them with his arms open, grabbed Serena, and pulled her into an even gooier kiss than he'd just given Jenny. Serena giggled and pushed him away.

"Natie!"

But he was unflappable. Letting go of Serena, he reached for Blair, pressed his wet lips against hers and sort of inhaled her entire mouth.

"What the fuck?" Blair exclaimed, stepping backward to free herself.

Nate just stood between the two girls, smiling like the luckiest guy on earth. "We're all too beautiful," he said by way of explanation. "I can't stop kissing us."

Blair met Serena's gaze. Yes, Nate was acting strange. He was off his tits, as they say in England. Still, there was something infectious about his puppylike exuberance. They'd just graduated today. Why not act a little strange? And why not kiss everybody? Some of them might never be together again.

And some of them were going to be together quite a lot.

"You want to see something really cool?" Blair asked, cocking her right eyebrow in a way that all the underclassmen at Constance had spent hours trying to imitate.

She stepped forward and put her hands on Serena's bare shoulders. Immediately, Serena understood what they were about to do. The two girls smiled, their heads drawing nearer and nearer to each other, as if in slow motion.

"You know you love me," they murmured in unison before their lips met in a kiss.

The room grew noticeably silent as everyone stopped what they were doing and turned to stare, but the two girls kept on kissing. Was this some sort of gag, everyone wondered, some final senior hoax?

Maybe. Or maybe not.

Disclaimer: All the real names of places, people, and events have been altered or abbreviated to protect the innocent. Namely, me.

hey people!

Good morning, graduates!

Didn't you think your face looked a wee bit different this morning—or afternoon, I should say, since none of us even went to bed until this morning? Yesterday was sort of surreal, but yes, it really did happen. We did it, and now we're *done*.

The days are short and the nights are very, very long

It's Tuesday afternoon—almost evening, really—and here I am still in bed. First thing I did when I woke up? Tossed my graduation outfit in the back of my closet and tossed my never-to-be-worn-again school uniforms down my building's garbage chute. I then thought about making complicated plans to take a bunch of friends out to the beach in Sag Harbor in my exquisite new European-import car. But then I changed my mind. There's absolutely no hurry. We can do that tomorrow, or the next day, or the next. So I ordered up breakfast from E.A.T., climbed back into bed, and here I am still, utterly content. I'm going to stay here for at least another half hour—until it's time to get ready to go out again. Forget frolicking in the sun all day—you have to get up early for that. Summer is really about those long, long nights out!

Yale club adopts new party policy

Twelve hours later and they're still scraping people off the oriental carpets in the lounge and tucking them into cabs. After last night's mix of topless girls, boys in human pyramids, girls making out with girls, boys making out with boys, the disappearance of the Yale flag that hangs over the club's front door, and guests complaining about the insanely loud music and cigarette smoke, the club simply had to do something. From now on, Yale Club members are welcome to throw parties, but only for other Yale Club members and their families. No outside guests allowed. Sounds like a certain Yale-bound threesome had better stay on good terms if they ever want to have any fun there again.

Looks like it's gonna be a summer of love

B + S

V + D

D + himself

V + herself

S + herself

J + some random but hot Czech artist who doesn't speak English

N + himself

B + Lord **M** . . . *and* herself, of course

But that just raises more questions

Are **S** and **B** friends now, or lovers? Does that mean the old hot-tub rumor is actually true?

Will **N** survive his summer of hard work and piety in the Hamptons, especially without **B** and **S**?

Will **V** get the *Breakfast at Fred's* cinematography job? How will she tolerate the film's madman director?

Are **V** and **D** actually together now? If so, will they last through the summer and beyond?

Will **D** learn to drive his vintage Buick, or will his hands be too sweaty to hold the wheel?

Will **B** really go to England to visit her handsome lord? Will she come back wearing a crown? Will she come back at all?

Will **S** make Audrey Hepburn look like an amateur? More importantly, who will be her leading man?

Will we still hear about **J**, even when she's off in Europe? And what about when she's at boarding school? . . .

Undoubtedly, you'll hear everything about everyone. I've never been very good at withholding information!

Not fade away

In case you're wondering: I may have just graduated, and I may be off to college in the fall, but I'm definitely not going to burn out or fade away. There's too much to talk about. There always will be. . . .

You know you love me.

gossip girl